SUMMER HILL INN

SARAH ALTMAN

This is a work of fiction. The events and characters described herein are imaginary and are not intended to refer to specific places or living persons. The opinions expressed in this manuscript are solely the opinions of the author and do not represent the opinions or thoughts of the publisher. The author has represented and warranted full ownership and/or legal right to publish all the materials in this book.

Summer Hill Inn
All Rights Reserved.
Copyright © 2015 Sarah Altman
v2.0

Cover Photo © 2015 thinkstockphotos.com. All rights reserved - used with permission.

Scripture taken from the Holy Bible, New International. Version, NIV. Copyright 1973, 1978, 1984 by the international Bible Society. Used by permission of Zondervan Publishing House. All rights reserved

This book may not be reproduced, transmitted, or stored in whole or in part by any means, including graphic, electronic, or mechanical without the express written consent of the publisher except in the case of brief quotations embodied in critical articles and reviews.

Outskirts Press, Inc.
http://www.outskirtspress.com

ISBN: 978-1-4327-8815-5

Outskirts Press and the "OP" logo are trademarks belonging to Outskirts Press, Inc.

PRINTED IN THE UNITED STATES OF AMERICA

Dedicated to
My mother, Nieldre Sarah Gibby, 08/15/1924-10/12/2014

Acknowledgements

Thanks to my sister and niece who read the rough draft and gave me encouragement to complete the manuscript. Special thanks to my husband for his loving support and editing skills.

Preface

Truth is light. That which is false is darkness and cannot be truth. Many are eager in the beginning to look for truth. However, the introspection that is required for such a pursuit may create discomfort resulting in hesitation to continue, causing the faint of heart to abandon the quest.

When an individual decides to begin his search, the light of truth may seem far away; surrounded as it is by shadows that can make it difficult to discern between what is real and what is false. The soul may become tired and discouraged. The person may give up and decide that the bit of truth he has found serves him well enough. This can especially occur if the individual has stumbled off the lighted path and is in darkness (where the truth of what has happened [being on the wrong path] isn't evident). Therefore, some people only know small pieces of truth and some mix truth with falsehood, believing it is the truth and are quite unaware of what they have done.

The greatest deceit of all contains fragments of truth mixed in with large amounts of counterfeit philosophy (from the fallen world) enticing the person to dispense pat answers to life's thorny questions. These individuals may be black and white thinkers who are puffed up by their own self-righteousness. They have a tendency to look down at others, from their condescending arrogance, whom they believe are inferior and in need of their counsel. Or, they may be individuals who are prone to follow any new path offered to them without much critical thought of what kind of path it is or what the consequence might be if they follow it. If it sounds good or as if it feels good they will follow it until the next good sounding thing comes along to follow.

The road to truth isn't for the timid. It takes courage to honesty exam the self and to find the wrongs committed to the self and to others. The person must take the knowledge they find from continual examination and then be able to ask for forgiveness from others and to seek forgiveness from self. A person who seeks the truth must be willing to become humble, to realize that they are no better or no worse than the other person. They must be willing to go the distance it takes to find the next piece of truth, however far it may be.

Sometimes the way of truth will scale mountains and sometimes it will cross valleys. Trickery is in the shadows which can present many side roads, either seemingly straight, or meandering, none that lead to the truth. Only the Holy Spirit can guide the way. However, those on the true path will also find plateaus of rest in the mountains and streams of refreshment through the valleys to restore and invigorate. The wonderful thing about finding truth is that one piece will fit with the next piece helping the person to grow and become mature. Maturity brings with it peace and joy in living. This outcome from finding truth is available without respect to age.

The next few pages tell the story of three people, held together by family ties and circumstance, who decide to embark on a sympathy mission. The undertaking leads the trio down an unfamiliar road that produces a strange turn of events, causing them to question their long held fears and beliefs.

It may be possible that even though the path to illumination might be rutted and full of weeds, truth may be waiting just around a bend in the road, on a hill top.

Chapter 1

William carried the last of the dried supper dishes into the dining area and deposited them behind the glass door of the hutch sitting on top of the antique buffet. Hanging up the damp dish towel on the door handle of the refrigerator, he thought that it would be great and less work to have a dishwasher. However, he thought, as he went through the kitchen doorway and into the den, that with their old house, it would take some major remodeling of pipes and wires, to accomplish his wish. And, he concluded, major money as well. His last thought helped him to dismiss his original wish and decide that it wasn't that much work to dry the dishes after all.

Settling down into the worn and faded couch in front of the T.V., he picked up the remote and channel surfed, while the coffee dripped silently into the glass carafe. Martha continued wiping the bits of leftover food preparation from the counter top, while Will put away the dishes. The dual coffee pot on the decaf side signaled its finished task, prompting Martha to pour two cups of their favorite blend for their evening pleasure. William liked his black. Martha had long ago given up sugar in her coffee but couldn't seem to do without a little bit of cream to soften some of the bitterness on her taste buds. Both enjoyed their nightly ritual of coffee and a little TV after supper and before bed.

Martha brought the steaming cups into the room and put the appropriate cup on each of the two end tables on either side of the sofa. Martha sat down on the cushion next to William, kicked off her shoes, and rested her feet on the painted oak coffee table. Will picked up his coffee and switched to the Hallmark movie they had been waiting to see.

Fifteen minutes into the film, Martha heard the phone ring in the kitchen. With a sigh, she reluctantly pulled her self away from the comfort of the couch and TV movie and went into the kitchen to stop the incessant noise.

Martha glanced at the caller ID and realized it was her mother Nell. Martha knew that she might as well forget about being able to get back to the movie; she would be lucky if she could hang up after 30 minutes. Resisting the urge to let the machine answer, she picked up the handset and gingerly placed the phone to her ear.

"Hi Mother"

"Martha," Nell said loudly. "Terrible news, your Aunt Audrey's son Keith just died. I feel so bad for Audrey; you know that this is the second child that she has lost. She has had such a hard life. You won't believe what's been going on in that family........"

Martha continued to nod and make affirmative murmurs as she listened to her mother go on and on about her aunt's first marriage to an alcoholic and how each of her children had disappointed Aunt Audrey by never amounting to anything. Nell repeated the story of how her aunt had finally married Ed, after her first husband drank himself to death. Nell complained that this marriage was only a slightly better one for her aunt. Nell again told Martha that she had never really liked Ed. She believed that Ed had only married her sister for the little bit of money Audrey had received from the sale of their parent's farm. Now Ed was sick with cancer, not doing well, and was surely going to die soon, causing more pain for Aunt Audrey. Martha's mother continued ranting for what seemed like hours about the problems with Aunt Audrey's family, Keith's awful illness and who was going to be at the funeral.

Aunt Audrey was Nell's sister, one of only two girls in a family of 8 siblings. There had been lots of conflict between the children and the parents. And, Nell never missed an opportunity to voice her opinion about who caused what and who was to blame. Martha thought that her mother seemed to be the one who was always stirring the family pot. It seemed to Martha that nothing really got resolved from Nell's perspective, since her mother continued to bring up the same issues over and over again, causing Martha to cringe inwardly every time the stories were told.

Martha had heard it all before and frankly she was tired of rehashing family problems. But, she patiently let Nell wind down, after all Nell was her mother and she was really trying to love her as God loved His children. The relationship had been better this last year and Martha was thankful for the change. Why, Nell had even apologized for a couple of things that she realized had hurt her eldest daughter many years ago when she was a child. The apologies delighted Martha and so she didn't complain when Nell switched to her "mother" voice and told Martha that the least she could do would be to write a note to her aunt, unless of course she really wanted to help her aunt by going to the funeral. Martha sighed and again felt the responsibility to do the right thing, which seemed to be whatever her mother wanted.

"I'm not sure if I can go Mother. I will have to talk to William. I'm not sure if he can get off work and you know I don't want to drive the six hours by myself. I'll call you back after I talk to him."

"Well, see what you can do." Nell insisted. I'm going to call the rest of the family. I think we should all go and give Audrey some support. I hope you can arrange your schedule to do something this important.

You know you were always your aunt's favorite. She always asks about you when ever we talk."

"Ok, mom, I'll let you know as soon as I can. Are you feeling any better?" Martha asked.

"I'm still a little weak from that terrible infection I had. You know these doctors don't really know what they are doing.........."

Martha, having successfully changed the subject, now had to listen patiently and hope that Nell wouldn't go on for too long. Nell was getting along in years and like a lot of seniors, she had suffered from some physical problems. Thankfully she had a good retirement income from her many years as an elementary school teacher and was financially secure from some wise investments she had made many years ago.

After she hung up, Martha decided to call her sister Mary to share her feelings of never seeming to please her mother. Mary was the middle child in a family of three girls. After their youngest sister Joan had died in a terrible accident, a year and a half ago; Martha had made an effort to get closer to Mary. She hoped that Mary realized that tragedy could snatch either one of them away at any time, and now that one of them was gone, surely her sister would come around and also make an effort. Although, Martha reflected, so far, not much progress to that end seemed to have been made, causing Martha to decide to double her efforts.

Mary and Joan were inseparable when the three siblings were children. They preferred to play together leaving Martha out of the games and often making fun of her when she cried. Martha in turn had become a tattletale, always running to her mother or father to tell on Joan and Mary for some minor infraction, actions that didn't endear her to either sister. Martha never felt like she belonged to the family and often fancied, as many young children do, that maybe she was adopted.

Martha shook her head and chided herself for lapsing back into thoughts that had controlled her life for so long and dialed Mary's number.

After several rings, Mary picked up the phone. "Hello."

"Hi, Sis, I just got a call from mother."

"I know, Mary replied. "She called me too and told me that she had talked to you. She said that Aunt Audrey's son Keith had died. I knew that Keith had cancer but I didn't realize that he had gotten that bad. Mom said that he had been sick for a long time. Don't you think it was strange that he lived in Ed's workshop instead of the house?"

"Yeah it was strange. You know I visited him last year when I was in Raleigh for that work related conference. Mother had told me that Keith was sick so I called Aunt Audrey one evening to see how he was doing and she invited me to come over to her house. When I got there she told me that Keith was staying in the workshop behind their house. They took me out back to see him. Keith was in this single bed under a window in the corner of the workshop. There was a small TV at the foot of the bed and on the other side of the room there were tools hanging on the wall. A long table with a built in saw was in the middle of the room, and unfinished wood projects were lying everywhere. It didn't seem like a very good place to live. He looked awful, really thin and dirty." "When I moved closer to his bed, he grabbed my hand and showed me pictures of his little girl, Rosie. I guess he had been divorced for a long time. Did you know that I used to have a crush on him when we were little? Thank goodness you can't marry a first cousin."

"Remember how we used to play with him and Aunt Audrey's other kids when we went to those big family reunions."

"I remember", Mary replied, "you know Aunt Audrey's oldest son, George, told me that Keith refused to live in the house with him and his wife or with Aunt Audrey and Uncle Ed.

"I know, he told me the same thing," stated Martha, "George said that he brought Keith his meals to him every day and tried to talk him into moving back into the house but Keith always said he didn't want to because he liked the privacy he had in the workshop." "When I was there it was dusty in the workshop and Keith didn't look like he had bathed in a long time. There was a bathroom there but it only had a toilet and a sink, no shower or tub so he couldn't have cleaned up even if he had wanted to."

Martha continued, "I only visited him for a few minutes; I was uncomfortable and I didn't know what to say to him. I told him a little about my kids and then left as soon as I thought I could without insulting him."

"Well!" Mary exclaimed, her voice rising with indignation, "Regardless of his so called privacy, I can't believe that George or Aunt Audrey allowed him to live like that. He should have been in a hospital. Living in those conditions probably hastened his death."

Martha agreed, "I know. You're right." and with a soft tone stated, "I guess they just wanted him to be as happy as possible, and if privacy helped, well, sometimes it's hard to make someone do what is best for them. I sure wouldn't want to live like that though. Who knows why people do the things that they do?"

"I guess you're right Martha. But it gives me the shivers. Mom said you were going to the funeral on Thursday."

"Actually" Martha replied, "she mentioned it and asked me to go. I told her I would talk to Will and let her know. Do you think we should go?"

"It might be a good idea, Mary answered. "Aunt Audrey has had it pretty rough and you know Ed also has cancer, no telling when he will die on her. She was one of the nicest people in our crazy family. Maybe we owe her that much. I wouldn't mind going and seeing her and some of the other family members. I haven't gone to a family get together in a long time. Donald is gone on one of his business trips and I would love to take a few days off from working around this house."

"Why don't we go together?" Mary suggested.

"Well", I haven't talked to Will about it yet. I don't know if I really want to make that long trip and subject myself to all of them," Martha hedged.

"Hmmm, on second thought," Martha continued, "it would make mother happy and Aunt Audrey has always been nice to me. I guess we should stick together and help each other when there is a family problem or crisis, and the death of a child is certainly the type of event that deserves family support. William will agree, if I ask him to go with me. I'll check with him and call you back."

Martha hung up the phone and contemplated if she really wanted to go. After a few minutes, she went back in to the living room where Will was on the couch watching TV, sipping the last of his coffee and eating a piece of the Boston Cream Pie that she had baked yesterday. Martha smiled at her husband's love for chocolate and custard, as she sat down next to him and snuggled into William's arms. This had become such a wonderful nightly ritual. Martha enjoyed the physical closeness of her husband of 26 years. Their marriage had had a rough start, but the last 6 or 7 years had been a source of comfort and intimacy that neither had ever known before.

Martha closed her eyes and pondered how everything had changed after she had finally asked God for help.

William and Martha married when they were both 31 years old. Martha had been married twice before. She had 3 children from her first traumatic marriage and a son from a second brief marriage to an alcoholic. William had never been married but had had a few live-ins and several one night encounters. Both had been searching for love for a long time and both approached relationships with a break in their spiritual cup that they were desperately trying to fill.

When they met, Martha had her 5-year old son with her. Her first three had been living with their father for many years. She had been in therapy for the past 2 years, trying to sort out her problematic life. Therapy had caused Martha to realize that she needed to do something worthwhile with her life. At her therapist's suggestion, Martha had enrolled in the local community college. She agreed with her therapist that an education would have the best possibility of giving her a better future. She had just turned 29 and decided that she wanted more than a man to make her life ok.

School was rewarding but not the answer to Martha's quest for a happier life. She was ready to explore other avenues when a classmate invited her to attend church. After many Sunday sermons, Bible study, and prayer, Martha asked God to heal her. Accepting Christ, Martha then tried to live His way, as she now believed. She worked hard in college and made good grades. She didn't date so as not to be tempted to sleep with anyone. She continued in therapy and was uncovering childhood pain and working through issues that had kept her from gaining worth about who she was.

William had told Martha that he had wandered through life for years and had spent many of them lying on remote beaches using and abusing substances in an attempt to mask the pain that was just below the surface. When he became conscious that his current path was going nowhere, he gazed into the heavens on a particular starry night and asked God to take charge of his life. Shortly after that, he came back to New York for his mother's funeral and then went back to Hawaii, after several months of the same old people and places that he had lived with before, he decided enough was enough. Within a few weeks of this abrupt change in direction, Will packed his meager belongings, came back to civilization, got a job and began to put the pieces of his life back together.

Martha and William were instantly drawn to each other. Martha knew that Will was raised Jewish and was concerned that this might be a problem, as their relationship continued to get more serious. William had asked Martha to marry him a few days after he had professed his love for her and she had said yes. She was so caught up in her feelings for him that she hadn't really thought things through. Still, his lack of faith in Jesus often intruded into her thoughts and troubled her until she finally decided to call off the wedding. William was understandably perplexed and wanted to know what had changed. Martha told him that they came from two different worlds and that she didn't think it would work out. She didn't tell him that the real reason was because she was afraid that he would only become a Christian in order for their marriage to take place. Martha knew this was a wrong reason to accept Christ; she had prayed for guidance and only wanted Will to come to Christ through God's grace, not because she had used his feelings for her to persuade him to her way of thinking.

William had already made plans to visit Martha in North Carolina for Easter and asked if he could still come. He had stayed with Martha's pastor in previous visits and it had already been arranged again for this date. Martha agreed and asked God to help her keep her resolve about the breakup. Martha didn't know then that her pastor had given William several books to read and had been talking to him about his salvation.

Early Sunday morning, before Easter service began, William came to the church with the pastor and his family and met Martha as she was starting to hide the children's Easter eggs. He didn't pressure her about her decision and only asked if he could help her hide the big bag of plastic eggs filled with candy and coins. Martha agreed and wished things could have turned out differently. However, she knew that obeying God was more important than any human relationship. She felt at peace about her decision and was able to enjoy William's company as they hid all the eggs.

Later in church, William sat next to Martha. The sermon was about how Jesus was raised from the dead after he had died as a sacrifice for the sins of the world and how accepting Christ as God's Son and Savior for mankind, gave new life to the individual. When the last hymn was being sung, the pastor called for any who would to come to the altar. Martha was amazed that William was one of the first to go forward. Martha's heart filled with love for William and took this act of faith as a sign from God that it was ok to marry William.

After the service, William and Martha sat together

at the fellowship meal that the members of the congregation had prepared. When the time seemed right, Martha confided in William that she loved him more than ever and that she believed that God had brought them together. William was overjoyed and told Martha that he believed the same thing and that he knew that God had brought him to salvation to live a new life with her.

Martha loved making all the preparations for the wedding. She had never had a proper wedding before and wanted this marriage to be right from the start. She made her own wedding gown and a white suit for her son. Her sister Joan made all the bridesmaid dresses and Nell cooked up a banquet fit for royalty. Both of her sisters and several of her friends were in the wedding party. Her father had even called and asked her if he could give her away. Giving the bride away was a father's privilege and honor that he had not been able to do in the past for any of his children because of his and Nell's divorce, when Martha was a child. Martha happily agreed and felt that she had done everything right for this marriage to last forever.

Neither Martha nor William realized that each brought unhealthy attitudes and dysfunctional behaviors to the union that would later threaten their marriage. After a fairy tale wedding and short honeymoon the couple settled down into an everyday routine.

Only it wasn't pleasant.

Martha's son had a hard time adjusting to this new marriage. Will tried his best to win over this newly acquired child; he didn't realize that just because he loved his step son's mother it didn't mean that her son would love him or even want him to live with them. Martha had been a single parent since David was two and they had developed a comfortable routine. William coming into the mix upset everything. When David was seven, William approached Martha about making David his official son by proceeding with an adoption. Martha thought it was a grand idea and believed that it would be the answer to making their family complete, besides she mused, it wasn't as if David's father really cared. He rarely saw his son since he had remarried and had gained a new infant daughter. David's father agreed. Martha and William drove David to Atlanta and spent the day at Six Flags over Georgia. After a meal of hamburgers and fries William and Martha explained the process of adoption to David and how it would bring their family together because everyone would have the same last name. Young David approved of the idea. He was aware that his name was different and he was tired of explaining to his friends how William wasn't his real dad.

The following year Martha became pregnant and delivered an eight and a half pound boy. William was thrilled to have another son. However, Martha was once again changing diapers and trying to lose her baby weight. Gone were the intimate talks that had first drawn Martha to William. There was less time to be together and Martha couldn't remember the last time they had spent the day exploring new places or just having some fun as a family. David was growing up, moving away from the closeness they had once shared; he was spending more time pursuing sports activities or playing with his friends. Working fulltime and caring for a new baby, who was now a toddler, added more stress to Martha provoking her to become even more critical toward Will. Often Martha would stomp through the house complaining, picking up toys and other clutter, and yelling that she had to do everything. William tried to stay out of her way by burying his nose in a book or by watching a TV program. Will's quiet gentleness infuriated Martha. She frequently upbraided him about his inability to get things done on her timetable or for the hours he sat reading a book, oblivious to her needs or the needs of their two children. William would often storm out of the house in search of some peace and quiet only to return home and have the whole cycle start again.

Once they separated for several weeks, but William's resolve to make it work convinced Martha to try again. However, nothing had changed in the brief time apart and they were both miserable. Martha asked God many times why she was so unhappy, she question God's supposed sign to her that she could marry William. She didn't realize that her unhealthy attitudes about marriage and her inability to be accepting of William was one of the causes of their many problems. She continued instead to try to mold him into her idea of the perfect husband. Now she wondered why she had married at all, only to make the same mistake again.

Martha wanted the marriage to work, she had been divorced before and it hadn't made her happy. She knew that divorce would only bring a different set of problems and that if she and William separated it would harm their two children. Besides, after years of listening to Sunday sermons about God's design for marriage, Martha now believed that God hated divorce and that it should be a last resort. She kept trying to make it better but nothing seemed to work and she felt at the end of her rope.

After 16 years of constant fights and resentments, Martha gave up. She had tried everything; nothing had worked. All of her talking, cajoling, and trying to convince William of what he needed to do, in order for the marriage to work, fell on deaf ears and glazed over eyes. It never occurred to Martha that maybe she needed to change. Martha told God that she just couldn't do it anymore, if anything was going to change it would have to be God's doing. She didn't know it at the time but giving up was the sanest thing she would ever do.

During this time Will was also struggling and had decided to get some professional help. Slowly things started changing. God was teaching Martha what loving someone was really about and how to give that love to her husband. Martha learned to keep her mouth shut every time she wanted to criticize William for whatever he did or didn't do that she didn't like. She learned to focus on all of William's good qualities that she fell in love with instead of his faults. She began telling William thank you whenever she appreciated what he did, like taking out the garbage or helping her wash the dishes. Martha prayed that God would help her husband to have a better life. In short, Martha began to realize that she needed to approach William with less criticism and with more appreciation. She began to learn who William was, what he liked, what he disliked, what were his needs and how could she be more considerate and loving.

William bloomed under the loving respect that Martha was learning to give him. He became more affectionate, withdrew less into his own world and was more aware of his and Martha's needs.

The last few years had been wonderful. They had

bought their dream home, both were settled into their careers, and their youngest son had married and left home. Now, after the day's work was done, both enjoyed a couple of hours of being with each other.

Somewhat reluctant to break the wonder of the moment, Martha softly approached her husband.

"Hon."

"Hmmm?"

"I just got off the phone with mother."

"Uh huh."

"Keith died."

"Oh, that's too bad.'

"I also talked to Mary."

Will muted the TV and turned toward Martha.

Martha met her husband's eyes and asked gently. "What do you think about going to his funeral? We could stop at South Carolina and pick up my sister on our way. Mary thought it might be a good idea to be there for Aunt Audrey. Mother's going. I'm not sure how I feel about going but it might be the best thing to do and it would give me a chance to spend some time with Mary."

"When is it?"

"Four o'clock Thursday afternoon." Martha paused and then continued, "Can you take a couple of days off from work?"

Will looked thoughtful for a moment and then put

his arm around Martha. "Sure, hon. I have some sick days I can use. I'll tell the boss tomorrow and we can leave Tuesday morning." Turning back to the T.V. he stated, "This movie is pretty good."

Martha snuggled closer to Will and smiled. He was such a sweetie. Her heart swelled with love for the partner that she had been blessed with. Her mind was no longer on the movie and she marveled at how God had taught her how to love not only her husband but also how to use the same process with her children and how she was slowly learning how to love her mother. Learning how to love others had brought so many rewards to Martha. She had learned how to give love and how to receive love. It had been difficult trying to undo a lifetime of trying to control others, who (she had thought), never seemed to be as responsible or as willing to help others, as she was. Martha had learned that control was an illusion; it had taken over ten years of therapy and 12 step groups for her to move that fact from her brain to her heart and sometimes she still failed, but it was well worth the effort.

She had shared the process with many of her clients in her private counseling practice and with some of the community college students where she taught undergraduate Human Service classes. Teaching a course in substance abuse counseling and how to work with people who were trapped in the addictive cycle of substance abuse lent itself well to teaching Agape, the Greek word for love that meant, "I will do what's best for you regardless of how I feel." The students understood that this kind of love was the best to give for working with hurting people and that this kind of love wasn't an emotion but an act of the will.

Martha often disclosed information about her own personal growth in the classroom, endeavoring to help the students become better human service workers and healthier individuals. Some of the brightest would apply what they had learned in class to their private lives and visibly become more accepting of others and more confident in themselves, reinforcing Martha's belief that teaching was the vocation that she was best suited for.

Before Martha knew it the movie was over. William shut off the TV and stood up. Stretching his arms above his head and yawning, he announced that it was time for bed. They had stayed up later than usual. Sunday nights were often like that. Weekends were time for sleeping late, which always threw them off of their routine. During the week it was bed by ten and up before sunrise.

Of course this was the second week in May and now the routine was a little different. Martha taught classes at the college from the middle of August until the first week in May and then she was off for three months. Martha loved her job, but she equally loved the quiet days at home. Last summer she had written a self-help book and was trying to get it published. It was all about how she had discovered how to have a love filled marriage by what God had taught her. These warm days were filled with writing, painting and spending time with her 8 year-old granddaughter. She felt that she had the best of all possible worlds and truly couldn't count the many blessings that she enjoyed.

William and Martha's nightly bedtime routine included prayers for each other, their family and others that might be facing difficulty. After prayers, they climbed into bed and settled in for the night. As Martha drifted off to sleep she considered how her life had turned out. It had been a long road but Martha now in her fifties believed that she had finally arrived at her destination. Gone were the terrible days of worry and pain. She saw herself as being a long way from the little frightened wisp of a girl who so desperately searched for love in all the wrong places. She finally understood how much God loved and cared for her. She decided that she could rest now and enjoy the rest of her life.

Martha had no way of knowing that the next 72 hours would shake her complacency to the core. She would find out how much more she needed to learn about herself and how the forces of evil would vie for her soul. Her next journey would be one that she would never forget.

Chapter 2

Will opened his eyes and looked at his watch on the night stand. 5:10, just 20 minutes until the alarm would ring. He felt tired and never thought that he got enough sleep, especially on a Monday morning. With a sigh, he decided he might as well get up and get going; the extra 20 minutes would give him some quiet time after breakfast, to drink a second cup of coffee and to start the new mystery that he had picked up at the library.

Shutting off the alarm, Will sat up, swung his legs over the side of the bed and stretched. Sliding his feet into his slippers, he stood up and glanced over to the other side of the bed. Martha laid with her legs curled up on her right side, still fast asleep. William marveled at how much he loved his wife. It wasn't always so. They had had a rough start, and at one point he wondered how he could have gotten entangled with such a shrew. His parents had stayed together through thick and thin, mostly thin, and he grew up to believe that you stayed together no matter what. However, during those first few years, his marriage to Martha had tried his patience and questioned his beliefs on more than a few occasions.

When he first met Martha she seemed so sweet and sexy. She was perfectly proportioned and standing at only five foot, two inches, she seemed taller, until she stood next to him, with the top of her head barely reaching his shoulder. She had medium length dark brown hair with lighter shades of color streaked around soft curls that framed her large brown eyes and full lips. Martha's body belied her old-fashioned name. William couldn't help but notice that her long flowing skirt hinted at the curved outline of her legs and that she walked with a subtle sway to her hips. Martha was like most women he was attracted too, smart, pretty and seductive; he was immediately drawn to her.

After a few dates he realized that there was something different about Martha that he hadn't encountered before which only made him want her more. She had refused to sleep with him even though he knew deep down that she was as interested in the prospect as he was.

At first it was maddening. After all, he reasoned, they were both adults and neither had been virginal for a long time. Martha had been married before and had parented children. She certainly knew the way of the male-female relationship. Will, on the other hand, hadn't married, (there had never been a reason to). He had enjoyed many experiences in the love department and knew how to persuade a female to his way of thinking. He hadn't actually come out and said any thing during their early dating days, but instead continued to put pressure on Martha by his physical presence and by the romantic overtures that he knew would melt a woman's heart. Still, to his surprise, she resisted his advances.

He had been perplexed about the situation until she made a statement that stunned him but also helped him to sustain a walk down a recent path he had chosen, one that he had started on just one short year ago.

While driving out to dinner one evening, Martha blurted, "Will I know that you want to sleep with me. That's not going to happen. I became a Christian two years ago and I have worked on turning my life around. God only sanctions sex in marriage and I want to do my best to obey God."

Her directness undid him and her message caused him to seriously contemplate where he wanted to go with the relationship. After some thought, he realized that he was getting pulled in deeper than he had ever been before; his feelings for Martha went beyond the mere short term physical encounter he had first planned on. He began to see this woman in a different light. He decided to behave and see where their time together would take the relationship.

Several weeks later William knew that he cared more deeply for Martha then he had ever cared for anyone else. He thought that this must be what love felt like. Every time they were together, he wanted to tell Martha his feelings but always hesitated, afraid of being rejected. Finally, he took the plunge and told Martha that he loved her, well, actually what he had done was to write the scary words on a scrap of paper and then leave it where he knew she would discover it. That way rejection would be easier than saying his feelings out loud and risking her potential "I just want to be friends" response. When Martha found the note, she reciprocated by expressing her own feelings of love for him. William was on top of the world and now more than ever wanted her. He began thinking of marriage. Maybe this was another way that God was answering his desperate plea for another chance at life.

William's reminiscing about the past ended as he shuffled into the yellow and white country kitchen. Martha was the decorator in their family and she had long wanted a farmhouse surrounded by trees. They had purchased this house with six acres of woodland five years ago. It had been fun picking out furniture together and searching for the perfect chair or antique chest to compliment the country décor. The house had a warm cozy feel to it that he loved.

Will closed the window against the early morning chill and turned on the gas log stove insert in the small keeping room off to the side of the kitchen. It had been warmer than usual for early May and by afternoon the house became a bit too warm. Opening the windows helped with sleeping but the nights were still chilly and by morning the house was well below 70 degrees. Removing the coffee from the freezer, Will measured the right amount for each of the two coffee pots with coffee and water. Regular for him, he needed the caffeine jolt in the morning, and decaf for Martha.

While the coffee was brewing, William went into the second bathroom and turned on the shower. Stepping under the warmth and sound of the steady spray lulled him into memories before Martha, memories of that other path.

The water reminded him of the beach. He had always loved the sounds of the surf and the feel of sand beneath his feet. That might not have been the reason why he had landed in Hawaii many years ago but it could have been one of the reasons he stayed for five years. The road that took him there was a long and painful one; one that was filled with memories that he didn't often allow to intrude on his now peaceful and comfortable life. On this day, however, he was willing to explore where he had been and where God had directed him.

Growing up in New York City as a frail red headed Jewish boy wasn't the best start for anyone and not for William in particular. He remembered the feelings of shame and embarrassment he felt when the local children taunted him and called him Christ killer. Will was the middle of three children, the second boy. He believed he couldn't live up to his older (and he thought smarter) brother and he certainly couldn't capture the fancy of his parents when compared to his cute blue eyed little sister. William's father was an executive in a large corporation and was very involved with his children. He sent them to private school and made sure, by nightly drills, that each child knew the Ten Commandments and all the Jewish laws and regulations.

Will's mother was involved with the World Jewish Congress, American Section and was active in several social groups. It wasn't commonly known among their neighbors that she drank a little too much from the home liquor cabinet and sometimes got a little too loud at social gatherings. She doted on William's older brother and let her younger son know just how much he had to improve if he wanted to come close to Edward's ability to delight her.

Will was precocious and could read at age four. His apparent intellectual ability prompted his parents to pressure William to excel in academics, just like his older brother had done. The constant comparison to Edward had the opposite effect that his parents hoped for. Under the burden of his parents' constant comparison to his brother, Will determined to play stupid in the hopes of getting his parents off his back. Of course this didn't work and the only thing William received for his misguided efforts were relentless criticisms and prodding to shape up.

William wondered, as he reminisced, if his home situation had contributed to his slow descent into the drug world or maybe it was his own innate rebelliousness. Whatever the cause, he choose the path of least resistance and became dependent on what he hoped would bring him relief.

Will was introduced to marijuana in high school when he was 15. It really didn't do much for him, the first time he tried it, and he didn't understand what all the fuss was about. However, two years later, William was out with some friends and casually took a drag off the roach clip that was passed around. The home grown drug produced a delicious escape and he reasoned that he had found the elixir that would banish all the evils he wrestled with.

In spite of himself he graduated early from high school and went to work. During the next few years William kept his drug use to nights and weekends, until he changed jobs and was introduced to heroin, prescription pills and LSD. It was 1964. Will was nineteen, entrenched in the drug lifestyle and ready for the hippie movement. After a few years, at the ripe old age of twenty two, William dropped out of main line society and joined other disillusioned youth living in the New York communes called "Families".

To make ends meet, William learned the fine art of panhandling. However, this occupation didn't provide a steady income, so in 1968 Will started dealing. Losing more of his middle class values, he began the life of a drifter, traveling the country hitchhiking and riding the rails. Along the way Will met some who used him and others who befriended him, getting a street education in the process. The drug business proved to be lucrative but William was increasingly paranoid and for good reason. Several of his dealing buddies were arrested. As a result, in 1970 Will decided to get out of Dodge and went to Hawaii on a whim. It was the perfect place for the now aging hippie. He landed on a beach that attracted many others just like him. Here, Will could relax, socialize and use drugs to his heart's content.

William stayed in Hawaii until 1975 with only a brief visit back to New York when his mother died of a rare brain disease. During the five years of sunshine and no responsibility, William had the good fortune to spend time with a seventy year old retired business man who had set up his tent in the midst of the hippie crowd. It wasn't until much later that Will understood that Herbert Dills had made this stretch of beach his mission field and William was one of his students.

William spent many hours visiting with Herbert, soaking up the age old wisdom that his new friend had. Mr. Dills gave the young man a bible and invited Will to accompany him to worship services held in various churches on the island. William was awed that this man appeared to have the answers to life that he had been searching for. The night before William left for New York and his mother's funeral, he looked up into the star sprinkled sky and whispered a plea. "Hey Lord, do it for me. Do something after I come back from New York."

It was slow in coming. After his mother's funeral, William went back to Hawaii and stayed for another year and a half. During this time He realized that he was becoming a different person. Will began adopting a more traditional value system. The hippie, drug filled life wasn't as appealing to him as it had once been.

William was called back to New York in 1975, when his father remarried. Will was thirty; he knew that his life needed to be different and time was running out. He decided to stay in New York. Within a few weeks he secured a job and went to work. Gone were the drugs and hippie life style. As time went on, the drug induced fog lifted from his brain, and he woke up to reality and became more willing to face his past emotional demons. This beginning decision set in motion his future choices.

William wiped the water out of his eyes and shook the memories out of his head. Turning off the water that had now become lukewarm; he stepped out on the cold floor, shivered and wrapped his body in a large white towel. Briskly rubbing his hair, face and body he began to feel warmth again in his heart. Putting on his robe and walking out to the kitchen, he glanced at the clock and went to wake Martha.

Chapter 3

Martha felt the weight of William's body shift the mattress as he climbed into bed. She had been awake for a few minutes and was listening to the breeze whispering in the pine trees outside the bedroom window. Leaving the window open during the night made a great sleeping environment but now it was a bit chilly. Martha scooted next to Will to feel his warmth. He was still damp from his shower and she breathed in the clean smell of him. William put his arm under Martha and drew her near to him.

"Good morning hon. Time to get up."

"Mmmm," Martha replied, "good morning, how did you sleep?

"Good, how about you?"

"I slept ok. What time is it?" Martha inquired.

"6:15. I've got coffee ready."

"Thanks hon," Martha leaned over and kissed Will on the cheek. She swung her feet on to the floor, felt around for her slippers and then slipped them on and headed for the bathroom.

Wrapping her robe tightly around her and crossing her arms against the early morning chill, she walked into the kitchen where the gas stove was dancing red and blue flames. She poured her coffee, added cream and sat down on the worn couch in the den. She picked up her meditation book and her bible and waited for William to finish dressing before joining her.

Sipping her coffee, Martha leaned back against the sofa cushions; closing her eyes, she contemplated going to the funeral and seeing all of her relatives again. Her mind wandered back to those big family reunions in the mountains and how much she had enjoyed being with her grandmother and playing with her many cousins.

Every year, in July, her parents would make preparations for the journey. After putting the family cocker spaniel in the kennel and asking the neighbors to watch the house, they would get the car ready for the excursion. The cooler was packed with sandwiches, fruit and drinks. A thick pallet of blankets and quilts on top of the folded down back seat of the station wagon made a soft bed for Martha and her sisters. Cars in those days didn't have seat belts to keep children safe, and yet Martha recalled feeling warm and safe.

Martha remembered becoming partially awake, when she was taken from her bed, in the wee hours of the morning, to the car. She would crawl in next to her two sleeping sisters and go back to sleep anticipating the long trip from upper New York state to Western North Carolina.

Martha's family would arrive in Clay County just about lunch time. Martha loved riding on the winding mountain road watching for her grandparent's farm and would squeal in delight when she spotted the white frame house surrounded by pine trees and wheat fields sitting on a hill. "Look daddy, there's grandma's house!" she would exclaim. Her grandmother, anticipating their arrival, would have the enormous dining room table spread with pork chops, fried chicken, her own canned beans, sweet corn on the cob, sliced tomatoes and cucumbers from the garden, mounds of mashed potatoes with brown gravy, applesauce and black walnut pound cake and the lightest biscuits Martha had ever eaten, loaded with hand churned butter and blackberry jam. Martha smiled at the memory. But, there were also bad memories of those trips.

They always left in the dark and her and her sisters would sleep until dawn. Martha's father wanted to beat most of the traffic and hated to stop for food or potty breaks. Whenever one of the girls would insist they needed to stop, Jack would promise to stop at the next available exit only to pass it by and lament that he forgot. Cries of "I really have to go to the bathroom, or I'm feeling sick" would cause an angry father to lash out with curses as he pulled to the side of the road and told the apologetic child to pee or vomit on the side of the road. Martha thought that she seemed to be the one who always got sick and felt distressed that she was such a problem. She wished for years that she could be good for her daddy. Tears welled in her eyes as she again felt the pain of those times. Wiping the lone tear that had escaped down her cheek, she turned her thoughts to the happier recollections of her grandparents.

Martha loved her grandmother better than anyone; she often spent long summer weeks on the farm staying with her mother's parents. Martha loved playing with her dolls under the graceful tresses of the weeping willow tree that swept the ground, hiding her from her own reality. Martha took rocks and spaced out rooms for her house under the tree. There was a kitchen, a living room and three bedrooms so her dolls could each have their own bedroom. There she could have the kind of family that she often dreamt of, a family without anger, curses or tears…..a make believe family.

And then there were the times when her grandfather would take her with him to gather up the dairy cows for the evening milking. Martha enjoyed these walks with her grandpa. He would listen to her running commentary about nothing in particular and patiently answer her many childish questions.

Martha stayed with her grandparents in the snow covered mountains of North Carolina for several winter months, when her mother and father divorced. That was a hard time for the nine-year old who had already suffered from her father's violent temper and her mother's inability to shield her from his tirades. Martha mused that it was probably better that the divorce had happened but at the time she just wanted her family to be like all of her friends with a mother and a father.

Martha was roused from her revelry when William came in, coffee in hand, and picked up his bible. Every morning for the past several years, William led a devotional for them. They would each begin with their own silent prayer and then each read their separate meditation books. "Twenty Four Hours a Day", for William and Martha read "The language of Letting Go", a book that had helped Martha to remember to let go of control and trust God to take charge of her life. This practice had helped Martha to become more in tune with God's plan for her life and to experience a peacefulness that she couldn't quite explain if asked. .

William waited until Martha had finished reading her book and then announced which key scripture was listed in their couples' devotional. Martha read along in her Bible the passage he had quoted and then he read the devotional for that day.

After all the readings Will bowed his head and thanked God for His many blessings. He prayed for

Martha, other members of their family, and for those they knew were in need. Martha finished their time by also thanking God for His provision for their needs, praying for William and other family members. Today, she also prayed for her students, who were on summer break and for two church members who had requested prayer.

This daily time together reading and praying had become a custom that brought William and Martha closer to each other and also to God. It was the reason they got up so early during the week. Martha felt that the time they spent together reading scripture and praying to God grounded her and made the beginning of her day full of the good that kept her on right path.

After Will left for work, Martha showered and dressed in her old black sweat pants and a yellow t-shirt. She walked down the hall, into what was once a bedroom for a long ago family that she had converted into a sewing room. She had always wanted a room where she could sew, paint and experiment with different craft projects. Before buying this wonderful house, she would have had to drag the sewing machine from a closet and set it up on the dining room table or bring out her box of artist's materials from another room only to put every thing away for dinner or some other family related activity. Now whenever she wanted to indulge in some inspiration, all the supplies that she needed were at her fingertips, plus she could leave a project mid-stream and just close the door and pick it back up at another time right where she left off.

The old farmhouse was perfectly suited for such a transformation. This particular room was painted a soft buttery hue with colonial blue ruffles that framed the eight paned windows. Each of the windows had functional blinds that could be opened to the morning light or closed to cool the room on a summer afternoon. Today, Martha pulled the blinds up to the top of the windows to view the pale green spring leaves sprouting everywhere.

Martha brought down the black and white fabric with the geometric print from the shelf in the closet and began making floor pillows for her oldest son's new apartment. Her son had recently separated from his wife of 10 years and had just moved into his own place. Martha was having a hard time with this recent split. She loved them both and didn't know exactly how to respond to either one. She understood why the split had happened and knew that both were at fault. Somewhere along the way each one forgot the love they first felt for the other and became critical and emotionally abusive, the other one responded by finding the acceptance and love they craved in another's arms. Neither thought of how their actions would affect their children or their parents. Martha surmised that a lot of their actions toward each other were accepted in the culture surrounding them and both had not been able to ask what God would want for their marriage. She knew from her own experiences that most marriages were doomed to failure (either splitting up or staying together unhappy) without continual contact with God.

Martha shook her head; she didn't need to go back in her thoughts again to that situation. It only brought her pain and confusion, especially where her grandchildren were concerned. She chided herself to remember that she had already decided to be supportive and loving to each child and to refrain from interfering. She said a quick prayer for each one and asked God to give her the wisdom she needed to maintain each relationship in a way that would be supportive and loving.

Martha picked up her scissors. As she cut the material and pinned the pieces together, she again thought of her grandparents. Remembering how each had given her the love and support that had meant so much to her when her parents had separated. She continually strived to do her best to give that same attention to her grandchildren; Martha hoped that it would sustain them, as it had her, throughout their lives. She smiled as she realized how blessed she had been to have such a great role model in her grandmother, one that once again was helping her deal with another difficult life situation. Martha was named after her grandma and she felt a special closeness to the gentle woman who had always managed to make Martha feel loved and important.

One of her favorite memories was when she was in the fourth grade and wanted to participate in the 4H cornbread contest. In those days children in that rural farming community were taught many skills in addition to the three R's, via contests and special events. Martha was excited about the competition and wanted to win.

After School, Martha kept wishing the school bus would hurry up and get her home. The yellow and black bus finally braked and pulled over to the bottom of the road leading to her grandparents' house. Martha was trapped in the narrow middle aisle behind her two cousins, who lived at the bottom of the road. Impatient at the delay, she was almost jumping up and down silently willing the pair off the bus. As soon as Martha could, she scrambled off and ran all the way up the hill to the farm house. She ran onto the screened porch, slamming the door behind her, through the kitchen and dining room and into the living room, calling her grandmother.

Grandma Wiggins came into the living room just as Martha arrived and asked her granddaughter what she was in such a hurry about. Breathless, Martha tumbled over her words trying to tell her grandmother about the contest. Mrs. Wiggins told Martha to slow down and patiently listened as Martha told her about the contest. Her grandmother smiled and patted Martha on her shoulder. She told her granddaughter that she knew just the thing that would get her that blue ribbon.

Martha asked how she could possibly win the contest when she didn't even know how to make cornbread muffins. Grandma Wiggins explained that she would tell Martha exactly what to do. Martha would make the cornbread muffins in the morning before school and wrap them tightly with aluminum foil. She told Martha that the foil would keep the muffins warm and that they would taste a lot better to the judges than the cold muffins that the other students would most likely bring to school.

That morning Mrs. Wiggins pulled out her brown stained recipe card and supervised Martha's first experience in making cornbread muffins. Just at the right time, Martha's grandmother pulled the piping hot muffins out of the old wood stove and wrapped the muffins together in one batch and sent the little girl down the road to meet the bus. Most mornings in November were cold enough for Martha to wear her heavy coat. But this morning, Martha didn't really notice the cold and felt very warm with the foil wrapped muffins sitting in her lap. Shortly after Martha arrived at school, she went to her 4th grade classroom and put her still warm package on top of her desk. Martha remembered that it seemed like an eternity before the morning pledge of allegiance was over and the intercom finished the usual morning messages by announcing that all the students were to come to the auditorium for the cornbread muffin contest.

Martha smiled as she remembered that the judges tasted lots of cornbread that cold winter morning before they tasted her muffins. Martha kept her fingers crossed when she recognized that it was her muffins that were being unwrapped and tasted... She noticed that each judge took a bite and then wrote something on a piece of paper. After they finished tasting hers, several more muffins were tasted and notes made on other pieces of paper. When the judges had tried all the muffins, they collected their papers and talked among themselves. First they said that her friend Judy was third place winner and a classmate, Jimmy was the second place winner. Martha thought that she hadn't won anything when she heard her name and was declared first place winner! Martha went up to the table and collected her blue ribbon. Martha took the ribbon home to her grandmother and kept it in her bedroom for a long time. Martha wondered what had ever happened to that ribbon. She decided that she had probably lost it in one of the many moves her family had made. As proud as she was at winning the ribbon, she was just a child when she had made those muffins, and hadn't been very good at keeping up with most of her things. Martha was grateful that even though she may have lost the ribbon, she had kept the many memories she collected while she stayed with her mother's parents.

Another memory of that winter, particularly stood out for Martha. It was one of the main reasons why she had wanted her own farm house, after she had grown up. Martha was mindful that she had been trying to get back to those happy childhood days her whole life. Buying this house was an attempt to recreate the feelings of warmth and acceptance she had always longed for but only felt in the security of that old home.

Martha recalled a particularly cold winter night on the farm. She had fallen asleep, while watching her grandmother's nightly ritual of combing out her long gray hair and then braiding it before retiring for the night. The room was toasty warm from the enormous fire her grandfather had made. And, the large brown vinyl couch, where she lay, had picked up the heat, making it the perfect winter sleeping couch.

Martha loved that room, especially in the winter. As night fell, Martha's grandfather always piled on several big logs to keep the fire blazing. There wasn't any TV at the farm house, but some times they listened to the big radio that sat on a small table under the window next to the fireplace. Martha used to make believe that the music she heard from the radio was being performed by tiny musicians inside the box, playing the elevator music that her grandparents enjoyed. On other nights Martha would watch her grandpa read the paper while Mrs. Wiggins crocheted or worked on piecing a quilt.

On this snowy winter night, Martha's grandmother woke up Martha and told her that it was time for bed. At the time Martha thought, "Why wake me up? I am very happy sleeping on this old couch in front of the fire, let this be my bed". But Martha Wiggins insisted that the sleepy child get up and go to bed. This was not a comforting thought. The fireplace was the only source of heat in that big farmhouse and the bedroom would be close to freezing. Holding the little girl's hand, Mrs. Wiggins pulled Martha off the couch and up to the fireplace.

As Martha stood on the stone hearth still warm and half asleep, her grandmother held a large blanket open in front of the fire. When it was good and warm, she wrapped it around Martha. The elder Martha guided the wrapped Martha to the closed door that led to the hall. Opening the door, Martha now awake, stepped into the cold hall. Mrs. Wiggins began to run with Martha still encircled within her arms through the cold hall to the back bedroom. There she pulled down the covers and Martha slid in, blanket still wrapped from her neck to her ankles. The weight of the many handmade quilts that were piled on top of her pinned her to the bed, so that she couldn't turn over. At her feet she found a warm brick wrapped in a burlap sack that her grandmother had put there before waking Martha. Mrs. Wiggins, tucked the covers under Martha's chin. Bending down, she brushed some stray hairs from Martha's brow and softly kissed her granddaughter goodnight. Swaddled with warmth and care, Martha's eyes grew heavy and she was soon asleep.

Martha smiled at the memory of those wonderful times where she knew she was loved and protected. Those few visits at her grandparents' house had given her all the love and security she needed as a child; love that was in short supply from her angry father and her emotionally absent mother. She remembered one very painful time, when her family was at the farm house on one hot July day right before the upcoming family reunion. Her mother was upset, although Martha couldn't remember why, and began screaming at her at the bottom the stairs to the second floor bedrooms. She began climbing the stairs when suddenly she stopped and turned back to look at Martha at the bottom of the stairs. Angrily she hissed, "I wish you had never been born." Martha's heart was broken. She loved her mother and tried hard to be a good daughter. It seemed to Martha that she must be stupid because try as she might, she always wound up making her mother or father angry at her. Martha's grandmother had heard the commotion and had come into the living room. Standing behind Martha, she heard the words of condemnation spoken by her daughter. Martha watched, tears streaming down her face, as her mother continued up the stairs and moved out of sight. Nell's mother came up behind Martha and whispered in her ear. "Don't tell your sisters but you are my favorite."

Those words sustained Martha through many more painful childhood years, two failed marriages and her readiness to enter therapy. Martha believed from that time on, that no matter what happened in her life, or who treated her as if she was worthless, she would never give up. Martha knew that she was loved by the finest person she had ever known and that said volumes to her about her value. She just had to find that value that was there inside and apply it to her life. Therapy had done that for her.

All of these wonderful thoughts and memories about her grandmother caused her to wince in self-recrimination when she remembered seeing her grandmother, over twenty five years ago, for the last time.

Her sister Joan had been the one to call Martha and tell her that her beloved grandmother was in the hospital and close to death. Martha had often thought of visiting her grandma but life had gotten in the way and she hadn't seen or talked to her namesake in a long time. Martha had stopped going to the family reunions after her first marriage when she was sixteen. Joan told Martha that she was driving to Hayesville the next day and invited Martha to come with her. Martha jumped at the chance to see her grandma one last time and told her sister that she would go with her.

It was difficult for Martha to believe that her grandmother was dying. Her memories of Mrs. Wiggins had been the one thing that Martha had clung to during the difficult times of abuse or loss that she had endured throughout her life. Martha used to tell herself that it didn't matter if this one or that one had knocked her down by dismissing her feelings or by stepping on her heart with their callous actions. Her grandmother loved her and that was reason enough to get back up and continue on. Martha knew that she had to see her grandmother before she died. She needed to tell her grandmother how much she cared for her and to thank her for all the wonderful things she had done for Martha.

Joan picked Martha up the next day. Neither sister said very much, on the long trip to North Carolina, each lost in their own thoughts. Martha knew that Joan also had her own special memories of their grandparents. She had told Martha many stories of her helping her grandfather stack wood, accompanying him to the store or riding with him on his tractor. Joan was a tomboy and the perfect companion to do all the boy things on the farm.

The patriarch of the family had died when Martha was thirteen years old and Joan was only eleven. Joan had lived with the Wiggins' from before her first year in school at age six until she had completed the third grade. Martha had always wondered why Joan was able to live with her grandparents for so many years. But, as was her family's custom, children were not told why anything was happening. Martha grew up with the dysfunctional belief that children were to be seen and not heard.

Rounding the last curve on the old mountain road, Joan pointed out the farm to their left, spread out in the valley. A tear escaped and ran down Martha's cheek, as memories flooded her thoughts, when the farm house came into view. Martha realized that this would probably be the last time for her to spot the familiar scene.

Joan pulled into the driveway and stopped, idling the car, as she looked for a place to park. There were several cars already parked next to the house and some were parked up the dirt road that connected the main farm to the house that Mr. Wiggins had built for his eldest son, James and his new bride Brenda, many years before. Joan pulled her car behind a red sports car, put the car into park and turned off the motor. Joan let out a deep sigh as she opened the door and slowly stood up. Martha deliberately seared in her memory the vision of the tall willow tree with its flowing branches touching the earth, and the pink and purple thrift (phlox) that spilled out over the front bank, before exiting the vehicle, as if this action would be a hedge against any future pain that would undoubtedly come.

Martha gathered her strength and followed Joan across the lawn and over to a small dirt pathway that led to a screened-in porch. The house was noisy with lots of voices that could be heard in the yard. Martha and Joan went up the three steps to the screen door and entered the porch. Martha continued to follow Joan through the kitchen and into the dining room. Some of the older family members were seated at the table, where leftover food and used dishes lay scattered. Uncle Floyd stood up and hugged Joan and Martha, expressing pleasure in seeing them. Aunt Mabel, still seated, offered them something to eat. Both sisters declined, explaining that they had stopped on their way through Hayesville for lunch. After a few minutes of small talk about their trip, they managed to pull away and went into the living room to see the rest of the family.

The room was packed with more aunts, uncles, and cousins of every age. The noise they heard outside was the result of a dozen conversations going on at once, each seemingly trying to speak above everyone else. As Martha and Joan came into the room, the group greeted the sisters warmly with hugs, kisses and questions about their families and jobs.

Martha inquired about her grandmother's condition, sharing her desire of visiting the matriarch in the hospital. Several family members cautioned Martha about going to the hospital. She was told that her grandma was very old and very sick and that she didn't recognize anyone. Martha brushed off their concerns. She was determined to see her grandmother before she died. She belived that the old woman would surely recognize the grown up version of her favorite grandchild. Somehow Martha had to let her grandma know how much she meant to her. Joan took heed of their misgivings, and decided to stay and visit with her cousins instead of going to the hospital. She gave Martha the keys and asked her if she was ok going alone to the hospital. Martha assured Joan that she would be fine and was secretly pleased to have the opportunity to visit her grandmother by herself.

Driving the 40 miles to the hospital gave her time to steel herself for what she might find when she arrived. Martha drove around until she found a space close to the entrance. She parked the car and locked the door. Martha walked up the sidewalk and through the double glass doors of the small medical center. She was immediately assaulted by the smell of sickness and death. Quickening her steps, she resolutely walked to the lone elevator in the small hospital and rode to the second floor. As she approached the private room on the first floor, she took a deep breath and waited a moment before swinging wide the partially open door.

Martha stopped just inside the door. She hardly recognized her grandmother. Martha Wiggins seemed so tiny and the hospital bed seemed so big in comparison. During all of her childhood visits, Martha's grandmother had been a large and comforting presence that could always chase away her fears with a soft word and a hug. Mrs. Wiggins had been a woman who seemingly knew how to do everything and who protected and cared for Martha. This frail and bent woman didn't look anything like the person Martha remembered. Seeing her grandmother in that cold impersonal hospital bed covered with only a thin sheet, brought tears to her eyes and she wondered if anyone would wrap this now small piece of humanity in a warm soft blanket, as her grandmother had done for her.

Martha moved closer to the bed. Her grandmother lay on her side, bent over almost to her knees. Her eyes were wide open, cloudy and unseeing.

The woman child took her grandmother's gnarled hand. The elder Martha stirred.

"Hi grandma, it's Martha".

The old woman turned her head in the direction of her granddaughter voice. She blinked and slowly recognition came.

Mrs. Wiggin's lips curved tenderly in a smile. She gently squeezed her granddaughter's hand and in a voice barely above a whisper, she murmured "Martha".

As quickly as recognition appeared, it was gone. The elder Martha's hand went limp and she retreated back to wherever she had been. Martha sat for a few more minutes trying, without success, to call her grandmother back. Martha wanted to stay but knew in her heart that the one moment she had received was all she was going to get. She stood up, smoothed the wrinkles in her skirt and slowly walked to the door.

Looking back one more time, Martha left the hospital room, leaving unsaid all that she had hoped to say to the woman who had meant everything to her.

Walking down the long quiet hall from room 208, she could hear her footsteps on the antiseptic tile floor. It was as if the echo was mocking her for not being there for her grandmother, before sickness and old age had taken away the one person that had given Martha everything she needed to maneuver through life.

"Ouch!" The pin drew blood, waking Martha to the here and now. Martha placed her index finger in her mouth, tasting blood; she deposited the offending pin in the box. Setting the fabric aside, she decided she needed a break. She went into the kitchen, filled the kettle with water, set it on the stove and turned on the gas for a midmorning cup of tea. While waiting for the kettle's whistle, Martha picked up the phone and dialed Nell.

The phone rang several times in the empty house. Martha assumed that Nell was on her way to meet with the other members of the Hat and Coffee Club that she had started in her neighborhood. It was patterned somewhat after the Red Hat Society but Nell didn't like that everyone had to wear the same colors of red and purple. She was too independent to follow a crowd so she developed her own club.

The members got together one afternoon every week at a local coffee house for coffee and dessert. All the women wore a hat and each tried to outdo the other with embellishments that they had added. The time together was filled with stories of days gone by and lots of laughter. Nell lived alone since the death of her second husband almost three years previously and she enjoyed the companionship of the women that she had grown to love. Martha waited until the answering machine picked up and then left the message for her mother that she would be coming to her cousin's funeral and would see her then.

Nell was seventy three. Despite her occasional physical ailments she was as energetic as ever and still attractive. Nell stood at five feet, six inches. She had kept herself slim and was an impeccable dresser. Her thick hair came midway between her ears and the bottom of her neck. Nell had let her hairstylist talk her into cutting a few wispy bangs but the bangs annoyed her and she continually brushed them to one side. . Nell despised the blue-white curls that many women her age seemed to think looked fashionable. She had decided long ago to let her hair gray naturally; as a result, her pale white hair softened her angular face, now marked with the wrinkles she believed she had earned. Nell was short for Nelma, a name she had always hated.

Nelma Jean Wiggins, Nell had often told Martha that she wondered where on earth her parents had come up with that name. Martha chuckled at the memory and dialed her sister's number.

Chapter 4

Mary was in her back yard, surveying the flower bed that bordered her white privacy fence. On her knees and sweating from the exertion, she was pulling up weeds that had already sprung up in the middle of her climbing roses, which hadn't yet begun to bloom. She heard the phone ringing from the kitchen through the back door that opened onto the patio. Running, she got into the house on the fifth ring. Breathless, she grabbed the phone from the counter. It slipped from her grasp and dropped to the floor. She scooped up the phone and spoke. "Hello." Mary croaked in a whispery voice.

"Hi Mary, its Martha. What was that noise?"

"Oh, I dropped the phone." Mary explained. "I was outside and I tried to get the phone before the answering machine picked up and it slipped out of my hand"

"Oh. Did I disturb you? Martha asked.

"No, I was just in the back yard doing some weeding and trying to decide what annuals I wanted to buy today so I could go ahead and get some planted next to my red and pink roses." Mary answered. "Why, What's up?"

"I just wanted to tell you that we have decided to go to the funeral." "Can you still go?" Martha asked. "We plan on leaving tomorrow."

"I sure can, Don is gone on one of his buying trips, so all I have to keep me occupied is to play in my garden or get my nails done for the umpteenth time. I wish he could be around more. It is so lonely since Ann grew up and left home."

"Where did he go this time?" Martha inquired.

"California. He'll be gone for two weeks."

"Wow, that's a long time!" Martha exclaimed. "He's usually only gone for a few days at a time."

"I know," Mary agreed, "but this is his big buying trip that comes once a year and it is for several different areas of the department store."

"Well, at least this trip will give you something else to do." Martha suggested. "I know the funeral won't be fun, but at least we will get to visit with each other and see some old and new faces when the whole crew gets together."

Mary nodded. "I'm not looking forward to the funeral but I would love to spend some time with you and Will and I am looking forward to seeing some of my favorite cousins. What time will you pick me up?"

"About 2 o'clock. Will that work?"

"It sure will. I will put my trowel away and get started packing. The garden will still have all of its weeds when I come back and maybe by then I will have decided what plants I want to get."

"Great! I look forward to seeing you. It's been awhile." Bye," Martha concluded.

"It has been awhile." "Bye Martha, I'll see you tomorrow" Mary hung up the phone and put away her trowel and garden gloves in the potting shed at the far end of the garden. She came back in and closed the back door. Mary washed her hands and decided to clean the sink. Picking up the sponge, she dribbled dish detergent over the surface of the sink and scrubbed until there were no marks on the white Corian surface. Mary's house was spotless and orderly, she couldn't stand anything out of place. She was also quite a decorator. She used her artistic abilities to make her home look like a page out of Better Homes and Gardens. Mary and Don entertained often and Mary loved impressing her guests with her culinary skills. Mary was one inch taller than her sister but had a similar build. She like to kid Martha that she was the big sister even if only by an inch. She had kept her curly hair a luminous brown that softened her perfectly oval face. Even at forty three she was beautiful and charming.

Mary was a self taught artist and had augmented the family income during lean times by painting portraits and murals for rich customers. Mary's husband Don had moved up the corporate ladder allowing her to now stay at home full time. She loved puttering around the house and planning elaborate parties to further her husband's career, but recently he was traveling more and she felt an emptiness that gnawed at her.

Mary had started drinking a glass of wine in the evenings. The warm glow of the crimson liquid took the edge off her loneliness, but now her one glass had increased to five or six and sometimes more. Mary comforted herself with the knowledge that all the health experts said that red wine helped stave off an early death, whenever the amount she drank interfered with her well developed denial.

Mary went into the master suite. Standing in front of the matching mahogany chest, she rubbed out a tiny smudge that was on the front of the second drawer with the tail of her blouse. Satisfied, she pulled open drawers, first one and then another, wondering what to bring on the trip to North Carolina's capital city. Finally Mary settled on the bottom drawer. Searching through last year's shorts and shirts, and under her gym shorts, she found a green and white t-shirt that had belonged to Joan. Mary loved that shirt. Joan always looked so lovely in green. The color always brought out the green in Joan's hazel eyes and enhanced her creamy skin and blond hair. Joan had taken on the physical characteristics of her mother and was taller than her two older sisters who mimicked the darkness of their father.

Mary and Joan were inseparable as children. Mary felt responsible for Joan and tried to shield her from her father's angry outbursts and the neglect of her mother. Mary had taught Joan almost everything, from tying her shoes to what to wear to school to which boy she should date. Mary often did Joan's homework, without her parents' knowledge or consent, to try and help her in school. No one knew that Joan was dyslexic. When she didn't seem to be able to learn, the school told Joan's parents that she would never learn beyond the fourth grade because she was retarded. (A term, Mary knew, which was considered defamatory and no longer used in professional circles).

Joan didn't know the root of her learning difficulties until she was an adult. One day while filling out some forms to get her son allergy treatment, the nurse at the desk look at Joan's script and told her that she believed that Joan was dyslexic. Joan didn't know what that meant but soon found out. With her new knowledge and some skills to compensate, Joan managed to graduate from a community college as a registered nurse despite her learning difficulties. Mary smiled, remembering how the knowledge that she wasn't defective or stupid delighted Joan, and how intelligent she really was. And, Mary noted with satisfaction, a darn good nurse to boot!

Joan was a typical adult child of a dysfunctional family and had all the abandonment and control issues that devastated her romantic relationships and caused enormous difficulties for her children. She had been married several times and had lived with an alcoholic husband for over twenty years. It was after a terrible fight with her spouse that she had jumped in her car and went racing out of the driveway. She didn't look when she entered the highway and the eighteen wheeler hit her broad side. She died instantly.

Mary felt lost without Joan. She knew that Martha thought that now since Joan was gone she and Mary would get closer. She loved Martha but it wasn't the same. Martha always seemed so sure of her self and had gotten more education than her siblings. Mary didn't feel that she could be much use to Martha and wasn't sure how to relate to her. She thought Martha was a bit preachy when it came to moral issues and she was never shy about letting Mary know what she thought. What caused the most conflict between the two sisters was that Martha believed that her opinion was the right one and was all too willing to give advice that hadn't been asked for, which Mary abhorred.

Martha had seemed to mellow somewhat the last few years. She seemed to appreciate Mary more and wasn't so free with her belief that her way was the only right way. Mary lived about four hours away from Martha so they didn't see each other very often, which was probably the best arrangement for their relationship. Mary hoped that this trip would turn out to be more than just Martha talking and Mary listening. Maybe, they would even get closer and be able to be real sisters. That would sure help mend the hole in her heart caused by losing Joan that didn't ever seem to heal.

Sighing, Mary folded the precious t-shirt and lovingly smoothed out the nonexistent wrinkles; she carefully put it on top of some letters from Joan that she had saved. Joan was gone and Mary was lonelier than ever. Once again she questioned why God would take Joan at such a young age. She didn't speak these thoughts out loud, fearful that God would be angry. Maybe He was angry at her and that was why Don was gone more and more. Was God taking him away also? This was not how Mary thought her life would turn out. She had had so many plans when she was young, the biggest one being getting away from home and being her own decision maker.

She had not chosen the best route to freedom that she could have. At age fifteen, she lied about her age and eloped to Maryland. The marriage produced a child and lots of heartache. Her husband of only two years died of a heart attack. No one knew he had a weak heart, from his bout with scarlet fever when he was a child. After her husband died, Mary pulled herself up by the proverbial boot straps, learned real estate, and made a good living for herself and her daughter. Mary had learned the hard way that the only person she could depend on was herself.

She had met many men in her chosen vocation but none appealed to her until she met Donald. Mary had first noticed Don when she shopped at the supermarket down the street from her apartment. He was the only one of the managers that graciously listened to her complaint that the store no longer carried one of her favorite products. Donald patiently explained why the item was no longer available. After that, Don would always make a point of finding her among the various aisles in the store just to say hello. He was smart and good looking. Mary was captivated by his honest charm.

Mary enjoyed a whirlwind courtship of dinner dates, concerts and dancing. Mary especially loved sitting under the spreading branches of one of the old maples that graced the rolling hills of the local park, just talking with each other. Several months after their first date, Donald proposed and Mary said yes! Gladly giving up her independent single life to be with the man she adored. They had a beautiful wedding and a glorious honeymoon in Cancun.

Mary believed that marrying Don had been the best decision she had ever made. He was a wonderful husband, attentive and dependable. They had worked hard and had a lovely home and financial security to show for it. Now that they were settled and didn't have to work so hard just to keep the roof over their heads, Mary felt that it was all for naught. She resented the frequent business trips that took her husband away. Mary had spent so much time helping Donald advance in his career that she had neglected developing friendships that would have alleviated some of the lonely hours she spent wishing things were different. She had her beautiful home, lots of money to spend and wine to keep her company. It wasn't enough.

Mary left her packing in disgust and decided that she would finish tomorrow. It was getting late and she was hungry. She hastily put together a salad and warmed up some leftover pasta. The meal wasn't satisfying. Dumping most of it down the garbage disposal, she brushed tears from her eyes as she reached for the jug of wine under the sink. She took the bottle and her favorite glass and went outside to the patio. Mary sat in her lounge chair, sipped the cool liquid and reflected about her place among the garden flowers until the sun went down.

Chapter 5

Early Tuesday morning, Will and Martha woke up the same time as usual except that this day they spent a little extra time in bed. They knew the trip would take additional time since they would be going to South Carolina first to pick up Mary and then back up to North Carolina to proceed to Raleigh. Both dreaded the long hours of driving ahead and wanted to prolong the delight they found in each other's arms. But, sooner or later reality pokes its unwelcome head in everyone's life. So it was up and out of bed, attending to all the tasks of getting ready for the trip.

Bringing suitcases and a cooler down the steps to the waiting car, William packed the trunk and back seat with the same detail oriented strategy that was apparent in his occupation as a draftsman. Martha marveled that Will could pack an unbelievable amount of stuff in a very small space and still have room for items bought on vacation. Of course this wasn't a vacation, although Martha hoped that she might enjoy some amount of fun on this trip. Leaving ample room for Mary's bags, William declared that it was time to go.

He patiently waited while Martha decided she needed one more trip to the bathroom before departing.

After a several hours of driving toward South Carolina, Martha stated that she was getting hungry and wanted to stop. They had just about an hour before Mary was expecting them and were within only 15 minutes of her house. They pulled into a Shoney's and after being seated, both decided on the lunch buffet. During lunch, William noticed that Martha had been quieter than usual and wondered out loud what was in her head.

"Honey, why so quiet?"

"Oh, I was just thinking of my family." Martha replied. "I'm glad you decided to go with me. I don't think I could have taken this trip alone. And, you know how mother is; she would have thought I was a traitor to family values if I hadn't gone. You know the one she always repeats," "families stick together no matter what."

"I think you put too much stock in what you believe your mother thinks. You know, it is possible that she would understand." William interjected.

"I guess so." Martha agreed. "I know I need to worry less about what other people think of me and more of what I think of myself. I do work on it. It just seems that when I am under stress, I revert back to my old ways. I am still glad you came. I enjoy your company. You keep me grounded and increase my serenity. I love you."

"I love you more."

Martha smiled. This exchange was a pattern that she and Will had developed. Just like a lot of couples who have pet sayings, Will always added the word "more" to his declarations of love for her. Plus, she knew that he had to have spent lots of time scouring the rows of cards until he found the perfect one that ended with "I Love You More", to present to her on card giving occasions. And, when he couldn't find one with those words he would write them in the card. Martha was especially delighted when he penned a love poem for a birthday or Valentine's Day. Martha saved all the cards and poems he gave her and had framed some of them. Any person going through their house could readily see how much love was in that home.

After lunch, they drove the remaining few miles to Mary's house located in the midst of a tree lined gated community. Mary's house was impressive. It was a two story colonial with massive columns flanking the heavy wood doors, etched glass window panes on either side of the doors added a touch of splendor, letting in light while maintaining privacy. Flowers of every description spilled out over the window boxes under the lower level windows and brightly bordered the massive structure. The large manicured lawn with its carefully pruned trees provided the final punctuation to the overall picture of prosperity.

Mary met them at the door and insisted that they have some of her special lemon cake and iced tea before leaving for Raleigh. Over dessert the two women began discussing family matters while William sat back in the easy chair and closed his eyes. When the talk began to sound like old news that droned on and on, he dozed. He was awakened abruptly when he heard dishes being scraped and water running in the sink. Stretching, he stood up and brought his dish to the sink.

Martha took his dish and handing it to Mary, declared that they had better leave if they wanted to get to the big city before dark. Turning to William, Martha stood on her tiptoes, put her hand on his shoulder and softly kissed his cheek. She asked him to put Mary's suitcase in the trunk; William smiled at his wife, agreed to the request and kissed her back.

Will picked up Mary's bag sitting at the door. He opened the door and stepped out under the small portico between the massive columns. Martha and Mary followed and Mary closed and locked the door, putting the key in her purse. As they walked down the sidewalk to the driveway, a sharp breeze ruffled Mary's light sweater, causing her to pull her sweater closer and to fold her arms about her. Looking up she noted some black clouds next to the fluffy white ones in the blue sky. Commenting to no one in particular, Mary stated that it looked like a storm was moving in.

Arriving at the car, Martha opened the front door and slid in next to Will and Mary climbed into the back seat. William released the emergency brake, backed out of the driveway and headed for the state's capital. A few miles down the road, Mary asked Martha if she felt any better about going to the funeral.

"I'll feel fine if Mother doesn't give me any of her supposedly secret messages."

"What do you mean?" Mary asked.

"Well," Martha replied, "she tends to say one thing and mean another. Whenever I confront her about the message she is sending, she tells me that her comment was perfectly innocent and she can't understand why I think she has some underlying agenda."

"Mother really gets under your skin, doesn't she?"

"Yeah, she does."

"Maybe what she says is true."

"What's that?"

"You're just too sensitive!"

Both women laughed at the family joke between them. Nell had often complained that Martha was thin skinned and let everything bother her. Although, Martha knew that what Mary said was in jest, it did have a ring of truth to it. She wished she could ignore the little things that people did instead of getting so bent out of shape over things that other people would never notice.

Martha told Mary that the other frustration she had about this family gathering was being around her Uncle John and Aunt June. They had done well and loved flaunting their latest car purchase, or their expensive clothes and where they had gone on their fourth jaunt of the year. The other family members would hang on to every word that was uttered out of their mouths and they all seemed so impressed that often Martha felt left out, dowdy and unimportant.

Feeling somewhat exposed, by revealing more than she had wanted, Martha changed the subject by asking Mary how she felt about being around the dysfunctional crowd.

"Oh, how they are doesn't bother me so much." Mary answered. "I just feel like the fifth wheel around all the couples. It seems that I always wind up alone at these family functions. I hate sitting alone at somebody's wedding with no one to dance with. And, now I won't have any one to share grief with - if I start feeling any grief. It's even hard driving down with you and Will. Our whole country is set up for couples and I definitely feel the lack of a companion at home and everywhere else."

Martha interrupted, "I'm sorry sis. I didn't realize how hard it is on you for Don to be gone so much."

"Yeah, well that's life. At least I'm not alone at home right now. Anything is better than that. Say, Mr. less than talkative, what do you dread about this wonderful excursion to the family happy land?"

"Well," William replied, "let me think, hmmm. I guess it would be that I have to listen to you two."

"Ouch!" Will exclained as Martha playfully punched him in the arm.

"Really, Will, tell us." Martha implored.

"Ok, I'll tell you the thing that gets at me the most" Will continued. "Its all the noise and all the activity. I think they wait until I arrive to tell me that this or that needs fixing or can I move this into that room or can I carry in so and so's luggage. I feel like a work horse every time I'm around that bunch. It would be nice if I could just relax and be left alone once in a while."

Martha deliberately ignored the comment in her effort to be loving. She felt that William tended to be a bit lazy and mostly wanted to be left alone to read his current book instead of participating in whatever was going on at the moment. However, she also knew that she was a lot more gregarious than Will. She was always wanting to be involved in everything and everyone. This revelation caused Martha to consider that maybe it was just that her and Will had two different types of temperament, not that one way of being was any better than the other way. Martha was glad for this bit of wisdom that had come to her and also that she hadn't said anything that would have surely hurt William. She wished it wasn't so hard for her to accept others as they were, instead of thinking everyone should be like her.

The car took a right sharp curve, causing Martha to look up from her thoughts. "Will, where are we? Are we on the right road? This doesn't look familiar."

"I'm not sure." William answered. "It doesn't seem familiar to me either. I know we took a different road from Mary's house than what was a more direct route for the scenery, but I don't know if we are still on that road. I'll pull over and take a look at the map."

William pulled over to the side of the road and shut off the car. He asked Martha to hand him the map from the glove compartment. Martha silently clenched her jaw and complied. Unfolding the map he propped it on the steering wheel and furred his brow. He muttered under his breath as he traced his finger from South Carolina to Raleigh. Handing back the map he frowned and broke the news to the two women.

"I think I made a wrong turn about twenty miles ago. I need to turn around and pick up 15/501 to get back on track." Reaching for the key in the ignition, Will suggested a break that he felt he needed. "After we get back on the highway, let's pull over at a fast food restaurant or a gas station so that I can stretch my legs." Martha inwardly groaned. It was a long enough trip without losing time getting lost on the way. Now William wanted to stop once again. But, she didn't voice her complaint and reminded herself not to criticize.

William turned the key but instead of the familiar roar of the engine, the only sound anyone heard was a clicking noise. He tried again, nothing. He got out of the car and lifted the hood. After a few minutes he opened the car door and slid back into the driver's seat. Running his fingers through his sparse hair he sighed.

"I don't know what's wrong. Mary do you have a cell phone."

"Yeah, it's right here in my purse." Mary rummaged around for several minutes, pulling out several items. Her face fell as she reported her realization, "Oh no, It's not here. I must have left it on the kitchen counter." Then thinking she had the answer, she brightened. "Don't you have one?"

"No. "Martha and I have been discussing what plan we should get. But we haven't decided because they're all so expensive that we've been waiting to find the best deal."

Martha was irritated. She had been telling William that they needed a cell phone for just such an emergency as this but as usual he was dragging his feet about spending money. She took a deep breath and straining to remain calm said. "What are we going to do now?" irritation coming through despite herself.

William, feeling accused, stated, "When I got out of the car, I saw a sign back there against those trees. I think it was for a bed and breakfast. Let me go see what it says. Maybe we can use their phone and call someone."

Both women watched through the back window, as William got out of the car and began walking back toward some pine trees next to a gravel road. Mary turned back from the rear window toward the front seat and looked at Martha. Picking her words carefully, so that her annoyance at these turn of events wouldn't seep through, she put on her sweetest voice, "Didn't William check out the car before leaving?"

Martha heard the irritation under the false sweetness and defended her husband. "I don't like this anymore then you do but it's not Will's fault." Martha turned around and faced the windshield. After all, it was one thing for her to be upset at William; it was another thing entirely for someone else to imply that he hadn't been capable of doing his job. Will was almost obsessive about organizing for a trip and wouldn't dream of leaving without checking all the fluids and being sure the car was in good working order.

Will returned to the car and stated that the sign pointed to an Inn about a mile up the road. "I have an idea. Why don't we get a couple of bags and walk up the road to this Inn. It will be dark in a couple of hours and we still have about four hours of travel before we get to Aunt Audrey's house. I'm tired. Let's just stay the night and get someone out here in the morning. The funeral isn't until Thursday so we still have plenty of time to get there.

Martha and Mary readily agreed. The emotional conflict with each other over their predicament had upset them both and each thought that some dinner and a good night's rest would help to smooth things out. Will opened the trunk and each got what they thought they would need for the night. Will locked the car doors, and stuck the keys in his front pocket. As they began walking toward the gravel road, Martha saw the crooked sign and wondered what they were getting themselves in for.

The sign was tipped to one side due to what looked like some recent rain that had soaked the ground and loosened the stake attached to the mud splattered rectangle. The large black letters, now fading to gray, announced the name of the Inn. Connected to the former were two pale red arrows that informed the traveler how far they would have to go up a rutted gravel road for rest and sustenance. Given that the sign had lost its balance, the arrows now pointed to a puddle of muddy water.

Summer Hill Inn →
One Mile →

The road looked as if a deluge had recently flowed down the hill. The gravel was mostly at the bottom of the road and different sized ruts were gouged out of the dirt. Large Pine trees, Maples and old Oak trees stood on either side of the road as far as the eye could see. Tall grass grew almost waist high on the edge of the road while smaller weeds had encroached toward the center. The threesome trudged up the road, gingerly stepping around holes and areas of dirt that had turned into mud.

After a few steps, Martha stopped and rolled her jeans up a couple of folds to keep her pants out of the mud. "I'm not sure this is going to work. I bet this place is closed or abandoned. It doesn't look like anyone has been on this road for a long time. I'm sure glad I wore my sneakers though. Ugh! I stepped in a mud puddle. I'll never get these shoes clean."

Mary agreed with the forecast of doom as she took off her sandals and began walking barefoot. "You might be right. It does look pretty deserted. I hope you're wrong and that it's still there. I want a bath and a soft bed. And by the way, I'm hungry. I hope we can get some supper."

Will tried to sound optimistic "I know it doesn't look good but I don't think we have much choice but to check it out. Let's just hope it's open; otherwise we might have an even longer walk to any other place if we can find one. Watch your step, this gravel is loose. It must have rained cats and dogs to do this much damage to the road."

The weary travelers continued for several minutes, then climbed up a steep grade and around a sharp twist in the road. When they reached the top of the hill they were stunned at what they saw, each stood transfixed with mouths hanging open.

Chapter 6

There at the top of the hill stood a three story country Inn. The pristine white building was trimmed in a muted blue that competed with the clear blue sky for attention. A covered balcony fronted the second and third floors over the first floor porch. Entwined ivy and pansies decorated the open filigree of iron supports between the iron railings and roof of each porch that spanned the entire width of the Inn. The covered entrance, as well as all the porches, were littered with a mismatch assortment of rocking and straight back wooden chairs. On the visitors' left was a huge Magnolia tree not yet in bloom and on the right an old slat fence enclosed a vegetable and flower garden that already had a few shoots of green peeking up out of the rich black soil. Rose bushes grew along the outside of the garden fence that partially obscured the peeling paint on the wooden slats. White and pink peonies bloomed among the azalea bushes planted in front of the main porch. The front lawn had been freshly mowed, and an untrimmed forsythia bush next to the woods sprayed bright green leaves where tiny yellow flowers had been just a few short weeks ago.

The threesome smiled at each other. Martha was the first to speak. "Can you believe it? This is beautiful. Do you think they're open?"

Mary started across the lush green grass calling over her shoulder, "It looks opened to me, lets go."

Will slung his duffle bag over his shoulder and followed the two women to the front porch. Climbing the stairs, they noticed that the door was slightly ajar behind an old fashioned screen door, revealing a rich oak floor in the entry way. William called out, "Hello, anybody home?" No answer. Again Will called out. "Hello."

Mary whispered. "Maybe they are out back. Let's go in."

Pushing the door wider, the three moved slowly into grandeur from another time. In front of them was an immense oak staircase. Curving upward it disappeared into the high ceiling below the second floor. To the left was a large dining room, Martha walked softly over to the doorway and peeked in.

A stone fireplace that could hold logs of enormous proportions sat in the corner of the room. On either side were rows of windows that began about two feet from the ceiling and stopped about 18 inches above the floor. The windows on the front side of the Inn were open and semi-sheer white cotton curtains billowed in the breeze. Many tables, some with two chairs and some with as many as eight chairs were dressed in white linen and bright yellow cloth napkins. Real silver at each place setting sparkled and framed pale blue chargers. Small glass vases sat in the middle of each table waiting to be filled with summer flowers. Many tables against the wall held miniature kerosene lamps and some held candles not yet lit. Two crystal chandeliers at each end the room hung from the twelve foot ceiling. Martha surmised that the door at the other end of the room probably went to the kitchen. It looked as though the Inn was in preparation for a busy season.

Hearing footsteps, all three looked up and watched as a slender middle aged woman, came down the steps in front of them. She was dressed in blue jeans and an old white tee shirt but she carried herself and descended the steps as if she wore a ball gown and was making her grand entrance. Martha thought she might be about her same age or a little younger. Wisps of gray streaked hair had escaped from her drooping pony tail; her face was devoid of makeup but was flushed pink from exertion.

With a surprised look on her face, she cleared her throat, "I'm sorry, we won't be open until June first. I don't...."

Mary interrupted, "Please excuse us for barging in. We knocked but no one answered. Our car broke down. We were hoping to spend the night but can we just use your phone to call a mechanic?"

"Oh." The woman replied. "Our phone is out of order. We had a terrible thunder storm last night and the electric and the phone are both out. I'm sure both of them will get fixed by sometime tomorrow. We've been in the process of getting ready for our first guests that are due to arrive in a couple of weeks."

Martha felt crest fallen and looked to Will to decide what to do. Will apologized for intruding and told his wife and sister-in-law that the best thing to do would be to go back down the road. "Both of you can wait in the car and I will go back the way we came and see if I can find a phone."

A raspy voice came from a room on the right. "My goodness Patricia let these poor folks stay the night. We have lamps and candles. And, I'm sure Dora can find enough food for a few sandwiches. Haven't you already fixed a couple rooms?"

The woman smiled and raised her eyebrows. In a loud voice she called out, "Ok, Aunt Katherine." Addressing the travelers in a softer voice, "Please forgive me, of course you can stay the night".

Mary half heartily stated, "We wouldn't want to put you out."

"Think nothing of it. Sometimes I get so caught up in getting ready that I forget that I have plenty of time to get it all done. And besides, the reason we are here is to take care of guests. Please follow me. And, call me Pat."

The group turned to the right and followed the woman, now known as Pat, into a lobby that put modern hotels to shame. The splendor before them was remarkable. Windows here were just as tall as the dining room windows but were closed and adorned with heavy dark green drapes and sheer white curtains. Several couches and easy chairs, covered in different muted patterns of green and brown, were arranged in front of the windows. Old coffee tables and end tables were polished to a deep almost ebony hue. The walls were a soft chocolate color. The rich oak flooring continued into the room, softened by rugs that defined each sitting area. A large portrait of a stern old gentleman in a black suit was hung next to a closed door on the back wall. To the left of the parlor sat a dark wood counter that sported a computer, an old cash register and various pens and pencils in a mug that said Home Sweet Home. A black phone from an earlier era hung on the wall. Behind the counter, next to the phone were rows of hooks on which were dangling keys to various rooms.

A bony and wrinkled woman in her eighties sat under one of the windows in the only rocking chair in the room. Rocking back and forth with a slight grin spread across her face, she surveyed the newcomers and then closed her eyes. Her shock of white hair was pulled back in a tight bun at the nape of her neck.

Patricia turned to her guests and whispered, "Aunt Katherine."

Pat went behind the counter; reaching underneath, she brought out a binder and began flipping through several pages. She stated that there were three rooms ready, two had their own bathrooms and one had a bathroom down the hall. William explained that only two rooms were needed, one for him and Martha and one for his sister-in-law. All agreed they wanted rooms with bathrooms. Just then the door next to the old fashioned portrait opened and a short round woman in her late forties emerged. Her ample frame strained the buttons pulling together a print dress with large red and blue flowers and short gathered sleeves. A discolored white chef's apron with a bib and straps covered the dress but couldn't conceal too many meals and not enough exercise. Her curly hair was bleached blond and cut short. Rhinestone barrettes pulled her hair back presenting long yellow beaded earrings that swung as she walked. Empty blue eyes gazed out from a soft fleshy face covered with too much makeup, lipstick and rouge.

When the woman saw the man and two women standing next to the counter she brightened. Wiping her hands on her apron she walked toward Mary and smiled. "Well, hello" And looking toward Patricia, she asked, "We have company?" Patricia looked toward the three and apologized, "I'm so sorry. I haven't asked your names." Martha quickly offered, "I'm Martha, and this is my sister Mary and my husband William." Pat offered her hand, "So nice to meet you. This is my baby sister Dora," Dora frowned, "I'm not such a baby anymore. They would all starve without me, since I do all the cooking around here".

And, while shaking everyone's hands, Dora quizzed, "Why are you here? We're not opened yet."

Mary smiled and answered, "Your sister has graciously agreed to put us up for the night. Our car broke down and no one seems to have a working phone."

"Well then, I bet you are all hungry," Dora replied, "how about some ham sandwiches and cold lemonade?" "It won't take me more than a few minutes to get it ready and then we can sit out on the porch where we can relax and enjoy each other's company."

Mary was the first to speak, "That sounds wonderful, but could I get freshened up a bit first and then eat?" Martha agreed that she could do with a little bit of freshening up herself.

Pat gave a sympathetic nod to her female guests and took down two keys from the back wall and walked around to the front of the counter. "Come with me and I'll get you all settled; then we can eat." William, Martha and Mary followed Patricia into the hall and up the stairs.

At the top of the stairs, Pat walked down the hall to the second door on the left. Turning the key in the lock, she swung open the door revealing a white iron double bed on the left wall. A pink and white patchwork quilt framed a white eyelet bed skirt; a soft green blanket covered the foot of the bed. Between the bed and the door stood a white washed yellow pine night stand. Displayed on top of the night stand was a 50's something white glass lamp adorned with a forest green lamp shade. Across from the bed on the opposite wall sat an old oak dresser with a clouded mirror. A dark almost black bench sat under the window that faced the back of the house. A padded cushion dressed in a chintz fabric of pink and yellow flowers covered the seat. Two yellow throw pillows were leaned against one arm rest. Green Priscilla curtains tied back with pink ribbons brought a soft femininity to the room. A floor lamp stood over to one side of the bench and a small round table sporting a twin white lamp with a green shade sat on the other side. Looking past the bed and oak dresser was a door that stood opened, revealing a tiny bathroom. The view included a claw footed tub and a small sink with its pipes exposed.

Patricia asked if the room would be alright for Mary. Mary smiled, "It's perfect. I love the old fashioned bed and pink quilt. And, the window has a great view."

"Good, I'll bring you a kerosene lamp before it gets dark."

"Thanks, I think I will wash my face before dinner." Mary put her bag on the bed and closed the door as the three exited the room.

Pat turned to William and Martha, "None of the other rooms are finished on this floor, do you mine being on the third floor?"

William stated, "Anything your have ready would be appreciated, we know you aren't opened and we are grateful to you, for helping us out."

"Think nothing of it." Pat smiled and continued. "It's good to have some guests after a long winter with just the three of us to keep each other company. We love getting to know new people."

Patricia led Will and Martha to steps tucked under the ceiling at the end of the hall. They passed other rooms on the left and right of the hall. All the doors were open, except the last two on the right. None of the beds were made up and many didn't have curtains at the windows. The steps had a landing half way up and then twelve more steps bent sharply to the left. At the top of the stairs the group passed several rooms, all with doors opened, and then came to a closed door on the left about a third of the way down the hall. Patricia turned the key in the lock.

This room mimicked all the others with the old wood floor boards and antique furniture. The bed was to the right against the interior wall of the hall and two windows faced the bed. On the opposite wall next to the door stood an old chifforobe, large enough for a week's worth of clothing. Placed against the bathroom wall was a low dresser without a mirror. There wasn't a bench here. Instead two stuffed chairs both slip covered in a navy blue fabric, sat under the windows with a square table between them. A glass lamp in the shape of a canning jar with a white shade was on the table next to the June copy of Poets and Writers. The room was done in blue and green. A chenille bedspread covered the new blue striped sheets that were folded down over the faded blue spread. Four plump pillows, covered in white, leaned against a high wormy chestnut headboard that had been polished to a smooth sheen. Blue flowered cotton drapes hung to the floor. Dark green shades could be pulled down to block out the sun for a late morning sleep in. A large braided rug covered the floor between the bed and the bathroom. The open door to the bath mimicked the same claw foot tub and single sink that was in Mary's room.

William and Martha thanked Patricia as she left the room stating she would bring them a kerosene lamp and some matches in just a bit. Closing the door, the pair dropped their bags on the floor and sat down on the side of the bed. Lying back into softness, with feet hanging down, Will pulled his wife to him, "this sure feels good. Maybe we can try out this old bed later"

"Hmmm, at least there isn't anyone up here to hear us. But, I am pretty tired. Maybe some food and a bath will put me in the mood. I want to go to the bathroom and then I want something to eat.

"Sounds good to me, go ahead. I'll wash up after you get out." Martha got up and shut the door to the bathroom behind her.

Chapter 7

Closing and locking the door behind them, Will and Martha left the room and walked back down the hall to the steps and then down the second hallway to Mary's room. Martha knocked softly and called out her sister's name. No answer. Martha turned the knob and pushed. It was locked. "Well she isn't here," Martha quipped, "I guess Mary has already gone downstairs."

She and William turned and continued down the stairs to the entry hall and into the lobby. It was empty. The old woman, Aunt Katherine, was gone; only a washed out pink flattened cushion, from many hours of use, remained in the seat of the rocking chair. Will and Martha left the lobby and continued through the screen door and out onto the porch. There they found Patricia and Dora sitting in chairs next to Aunt Katherine with a table in front of them next to one of the porch's massive columns. Sitting on top of the table was a platter of crusty homemade bread stuffed with ham and cheese, a small jar of mustard and a jar of mayonnaise, a large bowl of peaches, a pitcher of lemonade, and a stack of plates, bowls and spoons, next to several glasses filled with ice. Martha saw Mary at the end of the porch with a plate of food in her lap, talking and laughing with a man a few years her junior. He wore a pair of jeans and a sweat stained t-shirt in the process of drying that clung to his chest and arms. He was dark from being out in the sun and muscular from hard work. His black hair was mussed and his blue eyes twinkled as he listened to whatever it was that Mary was saying.

Just as soon as Martha and Will stepped onto the porch, Pat stood up, poured each a glass of lemonade and invited the pair to help themselves to sandwiches and peaches. Martha, thanked Pat for the lemonade and picked up a plate and a sandwich. Looking toward the end of the porch, Martha inquired who it was that Mary was talking to. "Oh, let me introduce you. Tony is our all around handy man and gardener."

Martha deposited her drink and sandwich on a nearby chair and followed Will and Pat to the end of the porch. Patricia interrupted the conversation that was now almost a whisper, "Tony, I want you to meet Mary's sister and brother-in-law." As they approached, the man stood and offered his hand. "Too bad about your car, I'm not much of a mechanic but I would be glad to have a look at it in the morning." William stated his thanks, shook hands with Tony, and turned back toward the inviting spread of food.

Martha hung back for a moment, feeling a bit awkward, she gave Mary her stern warning look, but Mary seem oblivious to the message she was trying to send. Martha managed to get out, "nice to meet you," as Tony sat back down next to Mary. Martha turned away and walked back down, picked up her supper, and joined her husband, sitting next to Pat, Dora and Aunt Katherine

Eating a sandwich that to this day she couldn't tell you what it consisted of, she watched as Tony resumed his conversation with her sister. Martha wasn't at all happy with the charm that this gardener was obviously piling on thick as molasses. She hoped that Mary had informed Tony, (if that was his real name) that she was a married woman.

William was saying something. (Lost in thought, she had only heard her name) "What?" Martha turned to her husband.

A bit irritated Will repeated, "I said if you are finished, I want to go to our room and read awhile."

Reluctantly, Martha thanked Pat and Dora for dinner and got up to leave. Patricia rose also and stated that she would go ahead and get them a kerosene lamp and some matches as she had promised. As they walked toward the door, Martha turned and noticed that Mary and Tony were leaving by the steps at the end of the porch. Inside Martha and Will followed Patricia to the lobby. Pat picked up the lamp she had put on the counter earlier and handed it, with a small box of matches, to William. Thanking Pat and saying good night, both left the lobby and started up the stairs.

As soon as the pair reached their room, Martha closed the door and faced Will. In a fierce whisper she accused Will; "Why did you usher me off the porch so quickly?"

Confused, William answered, "What do you mean? I just thought we could spend some time together. We did talk about it earlier." Will put down the lamp and tried to take Martha in his arms but she moved out of his embrace.

"Will, Didn't you notice?" Martha asked, still annoyed. "The Inn's gardener was coming on to Mary?"

"No I didn't. Will retorted. "And so what if he was, Mary is a big girl and she can take care of her self."

"Honey, Martha's voice softened, "you don't understand. Mary is ripe for the attentions of a good looking man. She is so lonely, what with Don gone so much. She is very vulnerable right now and I think we should have helped by interrupting them somehow."

William sighed, "Martha, you can't save Mary from herself. And, I'm sure you don't want to be rude by interfering with anyone's conversation. You are not responsible for another person's actions."

"Oh, I know you're right." Martha agreed reluctantly. "But, it worries me that she will mess up her marriage and regret having a fling."

"Listen Martha," Will responded. "Number one, you don't know she will cheat on Don, number two, you can't control Mary's behavior and number three, remember your twelve step slogans: Control is an Illusion, so …"

"Ok, ok, I remember." Martha countered. "Let go and let God."

"You got it! William exclaimed. "Now, sweetheart, how about giving me some of that hyper-attention?" Grinning, William pulled Martha back into his arms. Tilting her face up to his, he gently kissed her on the nose and laid his cheek next to hers, breathing in the familiar fragrance of her cologne.

Martha sighed, realizing that William was right. She intentionally put her worries about her sister out of her mind, and willingly moved back into the comforting presence of her husband's warmth as his strength enfolded her.

Chapter 8

William lay sleeping, softly snoring in Martha's ear. Martha, wide awake, realized that try as she might not to dwell on her fears, thoughts of Mary kept popping into her head. She was worried that her sister was going to get herself into trouble. Tony was way too good looking and Mary had shared with Martha that she was unhappy with Don's frequent trips. Martha was sure her sister felt rejected and alone, a combination that spelled disaster.

Gently extricating herself from William's arms, Martha rolled over and as quietly as possible, scooted to the edge of the old-fashioned bed and got up. Martha tiptoed to the bathroom. She closed the door and looked intently at her reflection. She tried to smooth out the worry lines creasing her forehead and told herself that Will was probably right; she should just let it go.

Martha knew in her mind that it was none of her business whatever her sister did, but her heart said, if it was her that was in trouble, she would want her sister to come to her rescue. Martha was convinced that Mary was flirting with disaster. Will just did not understand her responsibility to Mary. After all, what kind of person would she be if she didn't look out for her little sister? Ignoring her better judgment, Martha decided to follow her suspicions, believing that Tony had made his attentions clear, and that Mary would probably be unaware until it was too late. She took a deep breath and turned on the faucet. After splashing some cool water on her face and coming her hair, she walked out of the bathroom, past her sleeping husband and left the room.

Closing the door gently behind her, Martha went down the hallway and down the steps to the second floor. This time when she got to Mary's room she didn't knock but silently turned the knob; it was still locked. Martha's mind raced with thoughts of why Mary wasn't in her room. All kinds of images of what Mary and Tony might be up to added to her determination to rescue her sister from the clutches of the charismatic gardener, who was certainly taking advantage of a lonely and beautiful woman.

Martha went down the stairs and into the lobby; she stood just inside the doorway and looked around; it was empty. Then out the door and onto the porch, also devoid of any human presence. Her deepening worry propelled Martha back into the Inn and up the stairs back to Mary's room.

She tried Mary's door again, the knob still didn't yield to her insistent pressure. Frustrated, Martha continued past Mary's door and walked down the second floor hall. She peeked into each of the empty rooms. No sister. Moving back up to the third floor, she walked back and forth along the hall surveying all the rooms. She turned all the door handles and looked into the empty rooms that hadn't yet been set up for guests. Some were open so that she could peek in and some were locked, adding to her suspicions. Everything looked either abandoned or inaccessible, (she was was a bit suspicious that the locked and inaccessible rooms were for some secret purpose) increasing her anxiety about the whole mess.

Martha started going over everything that had happened during the past few hours in her mind. The car mysteriously quitting, the trek up the rutted and gutted road, the Inn that looked at first welcoming but also somewhat intimidating, with its large old rooms and antique furniture, plus having to practically beg the weird sisters and the ancient aunt that ran the place for a nights lodging. On top of all of that there wasn't any power or phone service so that they couldn't leave even if they wanted to. And, now her sister had disappeared. Martha began to realize that all of this had some mysterious purpose that was designed to keep them trapped here, but for what reason? Were they going to pick off one person at a time? What were they planning to do with each of them after they had captured them? It was enough to frazzle any one's nerves to the breaking point.

Martha wiped her sweating palms on her jeans and walked one more time to the end of the third floor hall. At the end of the hall she sat down on the bottom step of a flight of narrow steps in the corner that she hadn't noticed before. Running her fingers through her hair, she cupped her hands under her chin and leaned her elbows on her knees. Closing her eyes, she tried to calm herself and gather her thoughts. After a few minutes, she opened her eyes and became aware of where she was sitting; she realized that these steps must go up to an attic.

Martha's curiosity about this new find energized her current mission to find out what was surrounding all the mysterious events. Maybe she could find out what was going on by exploring the attic. She looked over her shoulder. She was alone. Standing up and leaning close to the wall, she began the steep climb. At the top, she found a closed door. Slowly turning the door knob she found the door unlocked. Looking back down the steps she waited a moment and then swung opened the door. Standing in the doorway, Martha looked around the room trying to adjust her vision to the dim light. She closed the door quietly and moved into the room. Martha noticed a lone bulb perched in the middle of the low ceiling with a chain dangling a short way from the light fixture. Martha pulled. Nothing happened. Irritated, she pulled again, still nothing.

Martha chuckled at herself, how silly she was; of course the light wouldn't work with the power out. Annoyed, she left the attic and went all the way back down to her room. Once inside, she looked over to the bed and saw that William was still asleep. Walking softly, she went to the table next to the chair and picked up the kerosene lamp and the book of matches that Pat had given them. Tiptoeing out, she gently closed the door.

Looking around uneasily to see if anyone noticed where she was going, she went back to the corner of the hall and up the narrow stairs. Once again she opened the door, went in and closed the door behind her. She took a few steps away from the door. Kneeling, she put the kerosene lamp on the floor. Martha raised the globe and struck a match. The flame jumped to life, causing Martha to catch her breath. Adjusting the wick to a lower and dimmer flame, she picked up the lighted oil lamp and stood up.

Martha lifted the light above her head and surveyed the room. The mixture of the encroaching sunset and the flickering lamp gave an eerie feel to the room. Standing in the late afternoon shadows, she took a deep breath and tried to quiet her quickening heart from the guilt that increased it's rate. Martha realized that she was snooping where she knew she didn't belong. It was one thing to look in all the empty rooms to find her sister and another thing entirely to go into someone's private attic. She began to lower the light feeling contrite at what she was doing when she caught a glimpse of a strange and frightening sight.

A long wooden table was pushed up against a wall next to a dusty window with 4 small panes of old wavy glass that distorted the view outside. Sitting on a large shelf attached to the wall behind the table was an arsenal of weapons that could carry out a quick or slow death: rifles, hand guns, long bladed knives and swords. Without a sound, and fearing the worst, Martha held her hand over her open mouth and moved toward the table. A frightened gasp escaped her lips; there resting on the scarred and pitted surface were a pair of handcuffs and what looked like an ice pick. Leaning closer to the table Martha detected some dark brown stains scattered at one end of the table top. Martha couldn't believe what she was seeing. Then, a glint of light from the middle of the table, reflected from her lamp, caught her eye.

A rectangular ceramic box sat in the middle of the table. Setting the lamp on the table, Martha hesitated, and then she reached for the latch and cautiously raised the lid. Inside was what appeared to be some type of ceremonial knife lying on a plush bed of crimson.

The blade's double edge was about eight inches long. Strange symbols covered the milky white bone handle. Martha closed the lid with trembling hands and took a step backwards. This looked like a place of torture. Martha marveled at what kind of people would have an attic full of weapons at an Inn designated for guests. It just didn't add up, unless there was more evil here than she first suspected.

Fortified with a resolve to get to the bottom of whatever was happening, she felt obligated to continue her investigation. With a bit of relief, buried in the back of her consciousness, Martha could now justify her actions; she no longer believed that she was snooping but uncovering something threateningly malevolent. After all, someone needed to expose these obvious dark and sinister deeds. And Martha decided that it was up to her to uncover and expose the evil she was discovering in this beautiful but deceptive Summer Hill Inn.

Turning away from the table, Martha detected an ancient trunk that had seen better days, under the solitary window. Coming closer and peering through the murky glass, she saw an old barn at the edge of the wood that looked as if it hadn't been used in a long while. Seeing no one, she put down the lamp on the floor, knelt in front of the trunk and opened the lid.

With some relief she noted that there was nothing

scary in the antique chest, just a bunch of pictures. Getting more comfortable and dismissing that she was, in fact, again snooping, Martha got off her knees and sat down cross legged on the wood planks of the attic floor. Picking up a handful of loose photos laying on top of several albums, Martha noted that most of the pictures were of a much younger Pat and Dora and several of the same man in the portrait hanging in the lobby. Another photo was of a woman that could have been a youthful Aunt Katherine in front of the Inn. The rest of the albums revealed more of the same. At the end of the third album there was an 8 by 10 portrait of a beautiful woman sitting in a rocking chair holding a baby.

Laying the last album aside, Martha got back on her knees to inspect the inside of the chest, which seemed to have a higher bottom then that of the outside of the trunk. She surmised that there were a good 4 to 5 inches of difference. After some prodding and pushing she found a small cutout that when she slid her finger between the bottom and side of the trunk she could easily lift the thin piece of wood. Martha shook her head when she realized that once again there was something creepy about a seemingly innocent old chest that anyone might have in their attic. Lifting up the false bottom, Martha found two guns and an envelope with more photos. Martha picked up the envelope and pulled out the whole stack and began examining each print. She found several pictures of a young man in a plain wooden coffin, resting on what looked like one of the larger dining room tables, in the middle of the parlor. In one photo, six people dressed in black, surrounded the table. The old man illustrated in the lobby portrait was standing at the head of the casket. It was difficult to tell who the other four people were since all had their heads bowed but at the foot of the coffin was the slim figure of a younger Aunt Katherine holding a lighted candle.

The rest of the pictures were of guns, knives and a closed coffin. Martha was stunned at what she saw. Now more than ever, she needed to find her sister.

Martha's hands were shaking while she hastily put back the guns and pictures and the false bottom; she put all the other albums and loose pictures on top. She closed the trunk lid, picked up the lamp, and hurried toward the door. In the corner of the attic she noticed an old sewing machine and dresser next to it. Curious about what else she might find she went over to the bureau. Setting the lamp on the top of the dresser, Martha gingerly opened the top drawer and found scarves of every color. Other drawers revealed soft hand knitted sweaters and flannel nightgowns. Realizing that there were not any other unusual items in this corner she turned back toward the window and looked out. Coming from the barn were two figures. Crouching down and blowing out the kerosene lamp so as not to be noticed, she watched as the figures came closer to the Inn. She could just make out Tony and the old woman that Pat had introduced as Aunt Katherine. The gardener had something in a big paper bag and Katherine was gesturing toward the woods on the side of the Inn. Realizing that she might get caught she started for the door and tripped. Righting herself, she looked down to see what she had stumbled over. Peeking out at the bottom of a dress form was a hand saw stained with something that was dark brown almost black, a vision of a tortured guest, minus a limb flew into Martha's head. Right next to the saw was a double chain with a metal ball at each end spiked with needle like protrusions. The chain was fastened to a black handle about ten inches long. Martha had never seen such an implement of torment before. With a physical shudder, she left the attic and quickly closed the door.

Martha moved silently and cautiously down the attic steps. At the landing, and after being sure no one else was on the third floor, she left the shadow of the narrow passageway and walked hurriedly, almost in a run, back toward her room. A door slammed in the distance, causing Martha to make a dash for her door. In her haste she kept turning the knob while pushing the unyielding door. In desperation, Martha, close to tears, knew she had closed the door gently so as not to waken her sleeping husband and couldn't understand why the door wouldn't open to her. She finally realized the door was locked and reached in her jeans pocket for the second key. She quickly unlocked the door, went in, and closed it swiftly behind her, turning the latch. Martha leaned against the solid wood and forced her breath to slow down. What she needed now was William.

Waiting a moment for her eyes to adjust to the darkening room, she looked toward the bed for her husband. Not only was Will not asleep on the rumpled spread, he wasn't even in the room. Fear rose in Martha's throat like a knot and her hands resumed their shaking; she searched the bathroom, hoping against hope that Will was somehow there. Martha sat on the edge of the bed and put her head in her hands, she didn't dare call out for fear of someone finding her. Where could her husband be? Was he now missing along with her sister? Had he succumbed to some terrible disaster? Would she be next? She needed answers but each incident only bought more questions.

This hope of a respite, from a trip that Martha had only agreed on out of some sense of duty, (which so far had only brought car trouble and conflict with her sister), was quickly becoming a nightmare of suspicion and horror. Martha decided then and there that she was going to find her sister. She left her room carefully, closing and locking the door. Martha straightened her shoulders, stood as tall as her 5 feet 2 inches allowed and walked swiftly down the hall to the steps and down to the second floor toward Mary's room.

Half way down the hall, Martha heard voices coming from Mary's room. She slowed her steps and quietly approached the entrance. Martha noticed that the door was partially ajar. Soft murmuring sounds were coming through the opened doorway. Suspecting that Mary and Tony were up to no good, she moved closer, ready to stop whatever was going on. Martha stood in the doorway and gently pushed the door opened just far enough for her to see what was happening. What she saw surprised and frightened her.

Sitting on the bench under the window with Martha's sister was the younger of the two sisters that owned the Inn. Mary's eyes were closed and her head was on Dora's lap. The heavy set woman had one hand on Mary's shoulder and with the other hand she was stroking Mary's hair. Dora's head was bent as low as her body would accommodate toward Mary. Dora's mouth was moving, emitting soft sounds that only Mary could hear. In spite of her self, Martha gasped. Dora heard the noise and looked up. She stared for a split second and then a knowing grin spread across her face. Martha wasted no time getting away from what she had just witnessed.

What was going on in this terrible place? What was Dora doing to Mary? For that matter, why was she even in Mary's room. She had never seen Mary that close to any one, much less someone she had just met that afternoon. And, who was the young man in the coffin that had been placed on a table in the lobby and why were those people wearing black and standing around his casket holding candles? And, why were there knives and guns and a torture table in the attic. Fear rose in her heart. She wasn't imagining things. Something evil was here, something satanic.

Martha had learned a little about Satanism and the people who worshiped the evil angel when she did a talk for a local service club in the 90's. There had been a big scare in the little mountain town where she lived when some kids were caught sacrificing cats and puppies during their religious rituals. The teens had been meeting in an abandoned and broken down church for several months. Citizens were in an uproar over the arrests and were demanding that something be done.

Martha, a teacher at the local community college where she taught in the Human Services Department, had been asked to do a series of talks for several community clubs. In preparation, she had researched the phenomenon through library resources and by reading everything she could get her hands on. She also attended a workshop at the neighboring county high school that was put on by several law enforcement personnel. Martha learned that kids were experimenting with the evil worship because of the popular death metal music that had sparked their curiosity. Her son had been a teenager at the time and she wanted to be sure he wasn't involved. Many of the things she had witnessed earlier raised her fears that something similar was happening here. Martha really needed to find Will and tell him everything that she had seen. She desperately needed to get his help to rescue Mary and to expose the evil permeating the Inn.

Realizing that they might all be in danger, she walked back to her room to decide how she should go about getting all of them out of the Inn. Martha closed the door and not wanting to be heard, turned the lock as softly as she could. Walking over to the window, she opened it just a crack to bring in some fresh air to clear her head. Martha sank down in the overstuffed side chair next to the polished end table to think of a way to get out of the Inn. But she couldn't pull her random thoughts into a coherent plan; something was distracting her. But what was it? Every nerve in her body became vigilant. At first Martha couldn't comprehend what it was; it took her a few minutes to figure out what was disturbing her. And then, she knew, it was the terrible silence, so deafening that her ears felt clogged; the usual nature sounds were absent, not a bird, squirrel or buzzing fly could be heard. Suddenly, a twig snapped, startling Martha out of her fearful thoughts.

Turning her head in the direction of the sound, Martha recognized Tony, now with a long sleeved shirt on, and the mysterious Aunt Katherine walking between the woods and the side of the Inn back toward the barn. As she watched, the old lady disappeared beyond the trees, while Tony waited, not still, but pacing back and forth between the building and the edge of the wood, his agitation clearly evident. Several minutes passed and after what seemed like an eternity, the thin frail woman emerged with what looked like two tiny naked men with bushy leaves for hair trembling in her dirt encrusted skeletal hands. Martha's hand flew to her mouth to keep from making a sound and watched as the two disappeared around the corner of the Inn. What was going on? Had the old woman conjured up some sort of weird kind of flesh, maybe to worship or worse, to sacrifice? Fear constricted her throat and she felt nauseous. Martha shook her head to clear it and took several deep breaths to slow her racing heart for a moment and tried to pull herself together. The sensible part of her knew that she wouldn't be able to help anyone if she panicked. Besides, maybe she was letting her thoughts get away from her. Pat seemed ok and maybe there was a good explanation of why Dora was in Mary's room, although for the life of her, she couldn't imagine what. And, surely bony old Aunt Katherine was too frail to harm anyone. Tony was another matter she definitely didn't trust the grounds keeper. He seemed to have taken far too friendly an interest, in her sister.

A few more deep breaths steadied her nerves and helped her to think more rationally. Martha pushed her anxiety as far as she could beneath her surface thoughts and renewed her determination to resolve the whole thing in an adult and calm way. Martha decided that she would go back up to Mary's room, she would tell Mary her fears and both of them could have a good laugh over Martha's crazy ideas. Just as she began to feel a little calmer, Martha heard footsteps, a key in the door and the latch click open. Martha grabbed the arm of the chair, stood up and backed into the drapes. Fearful of who or what was about to enter the room, she looked around for something, anything that she could use to protect herself as the door slowly swung open. Balling her hands into fists she waited. Will calmly walked in and smiled at his wife. "Hi Babe." He quipped.

Chapter 9

At the sight of her husband, Martha's resolve to be sensible crumbled and she burst into tears. Will was at Martha's side in two strides. Alarmed, he wrapped his arms around her, "Honey, what's wrong?"

With words tumbling over each other and between sobs, Martha told William everything that she had experienced that afternoon. Will, understandably somewhat taken aback, at first dismissed Martha's tale as utter nonsense but as she continued, he slowly decided that maybe there was something strange occurring. He had sensed a secretiveness or furtive undercurrent beneath the false hospitality that was offered to him and the women.

"Martha, slow down." William requested, handing Martha his handkerchief. "Maybe you're letting your imagination get the best of you."

"Will, I'm telling you." Martha said, blowing her nose, she continued still upset but calmer. "Something isn't right. After what I saw in the attic and in Mary's room and now how mysteriously that Aunt Katherine acts, I know that Mary is in trouble. Both Dora and Tony have taken an ungodly interest in my sister and we have to do something. I think she might be under some sort of spell or at any rate she has certainly been taken in by the lot of them. I know Mary. She is aloof and distant to everyone. I'm her sister and she rarely even gives me a glimpse of what she is really thinking. I think the only one who has ever been close to Mary was Joan. It's as if since Joan died, Mary closed her heart and threw away the key."

"What do you propose we do? William asked. "We can't just go barging downstairs, demanding to know what is going on and how Mary fits into the whole mess. If she is really in trouble, then we have tipped our hand and we will also be in danger."

Martha gripped Wills arm, in a frantic attempt to convince him, her voice rose, "We have to go back to Mary's room – together. We have to get her and get out of this place."

"Ok. Ok. Calm down. I noticed a flashlight in the night stand next to the bed when I awoke. It was getting dark and the lamp was gone."

"I know. I took it when I went up to the attic. Oh, no. I left it on the floor next to the window. I forgot it!" Martha confessed, her voice rising in fear.

"Hon, don't worry about that now." William tried to sound comforting, while he collected his thoughts. "Let's just find Mary and then we can figure out what we need to do next." Martha didn't reply. Thankful that her husband was on board. She held on to William, praying that this nightmare would end.

William grabbed the flashlight, and holding Martha's hand, they tiptoed out into the hall. Looking both ways, they silently descended the stairs to the second floor. Approaching Mary's door the couple noticed that it was wide open. Stepping inside, their investigation revealed an empty room. The bed was wrinkled as if someone had lain down on top of the covers. The cushions that had been on the window bench were now on the floor and the curtains had been loosed from pink ribbon tiebacks and drawn against the night sky. Mary's night bag lay open on the dresser with its contents spilled out on the surface. The drawer on the night stand was partially open. The whole room seemed to somehow shout Mary's disappearance.

Martha whispered, "I told you something wasn't right. Mary would never leave her room like this, much less leave without locking the door."

"I agree. Mary is the most fastidious person I know. What do you think we should do?" William asked timidly.

"I'm not sure." Martha retorted. "I just know we have got to find her! Who knows what may be happening to her."

"You're right. Let me think a minute." William suggested. "First let's go down to the lobby and see if she is there, before going anywhere else." "She may be talking to Aunt Katherine or learning how to knit. And, then all this drama will be over."

Martha, angry hissed. "William, will you please believe me! Something's not right. I need you to take charge and help me find my sister."

"Ok, sorry." William relented. "How does this sound? We'll go downstairs and try the lobby first. If she is not there we will search every inch of this place until we find her."

Martha, feeling better, silently nodded her head in agreement. Will took his wife's hand and led her out of the room and into the hall. Neither worried about shutting the door. It seemed pointless and the more urgent task of finding Mary was facing them. The pair slowly and quietly descended the last flight of stairs leading to the hall outside the parlor and dining room. No one was in either room. William looked at Martha with a questioning glance.

Martha leaned close to William and softly suggested, "I think we should go and look in that old barn. There is something very strange that Tony and that old lady would go there when they have no animals and the barn itself looks like it could collapse at any moment. I saw both of them coming out of that dilapidated building with something in a large paper bag. It may be where they have put Mary."

William shook his head and stated, "I can't believe I am doing this. I still think we might be jumping to conclusions."

"You wouldn't say that if you had seen what I saw with your own eyes." Martha exclaimed. "Please listen to me. I know that these things do occur, even if we don't want to believe it. You are such an optimist that you think everyone has good motives."

"Yes," William agreed. "And you are the cynic always believing that someone is up to no good."

"Well, maybe this time I am right." Martha stated. "At any rate, we aren't getting anywhere by arguing. Let's check out the barn before deciding anything else."

William didn't know how to dissuade Martha of her suspicions and had never been good at resisting her lead when she had made up her mind. Somewhat reluctantly (he wasn't entirely convinced, although some things certainly didn't add up). William stated in a barely audible voice his willingness to go and search the barn for his sister-in-law. "Ok, but let's be realistic and not let our imaginations get away from us." Agreed William. Martha shook her head, exasperated that her husband never seemed to believe her. It was like pulling teeth to get him to do anything.

Once more taking Martha's hand, Will took a few steps and carefully pushed the screen door open, thankful that it didn't squeak. The porch was deserted save for a large gray cat that jumped out of one of the porch chairs when the two stepped out into the night air. Startled by the cat, William backed into Martha, pushing her back into the hall. "Will, cried Martha, what are you doing?" "Sorry," whispered William. Martha stepped out onto the porch and looking around at the empty chairs, said, "See I told you, they have all disappeared." "Shhh," replied William as he descended the porch steps. Following close behind, Martha took one step at a time, reaching the soft grass one second behind Will.

Quietly, walking close to the building, they rounded the front of the Inn and stepped carefully along the side of the building, avoiding anything that might cause noise. They paused before the open field in front of the moon lit barn; Martha and William looked up and around to make sure no one was following them and then hand in hand they sprinted across the newly mown grass to the covered shelter attached to the barn.

Quickly moving toward the shadows inside the barn, William (now feeling silly about all the intrigue) tried one more time to dissuade Martha from going any further. "This is crazy. I'm sure nothing as fantastic as devil worship is going on here. Mary could be anywhere. Maybe she and Tony went for a ride or a walk, or something. If they find out we've been snooping, they will kick us out and we won't have any place to spend the night."

"I know we probably shouldn't be snooping under normal circumstances but why isn't anyone else around, and what about all those weapons and pictures in the attic? And the things, whatever they were, that Aunt Katherine got from the woods. Maybe this is crazy." Martha granted. "But, if it isn't and Mary is in harm's way, I would never forgive myself and neither would you, if we don't do something to find her and get out of here."

Exasperated, Will exclaimed, "Ok, ok, I can't believe you talked me into this. Let's go in."

Inside the dark barn, Will turned on the flashlight and slowly swept the beam around the interior. There were several stalls that had once held animals. Hay was stacked in one corner and between the bales was what looked like a new door painted a dark, almost black, brown in what looked like an attempt to have it blend into the barn's aging wood, but in fact it stood in sharp contrast to the peeling red paint surrounding it. William and Martha looked at each other, each with their own separate thoughts.

"That's kind of weird." William said softly, "Why would a new door be in an old dilapidated barn and where does it go?"

Martha, irritated at her husband's insistence to dismiss her fears and letting the irritation seep into her reply, stated, "That's probably where they hide the people they kidnap for later torture."

Will, visibly annoyed, replied, "Martha, I'm sure there is a reasonable explanation for everything."

"Well, William," Martha added, "if you have one, please tell me. I'm all ears."

"Don't be sarcastic. I'm just trying to keep our wits about us."

"I'm sorry", Martha said lowering her voice." I'm just so scared. I don't want to believe the awful things I've seen but the evidence is all there. You know there is evil in this world, even if most people don't want to see it. What are we going to do?"

With a deep sigh, William said, "Well, I guess we need to check it out. Stay close."

Slowly Will and Martha approached the unlikely entrance to what they feared awaited on the other side. Just as William turned the knob, the flashlight went out.

"Now what?" William exclaimed, shaking the flash light. "This is getting surreal and I am getting more nervous by the minute. Here take my hand we are going to find out what is behind this door, light or no light."

Martha remembered that she had left the matches

that Pat had given her on the floor next to the trunk in her haste to exit the attic. She didn't relish the thought of entering what ever awaited them on the other side of the door without any way of seeing what might bring them harm. In a show of trust in her husband, Martha grasped Will's hand and heard him push open the door. William reached in his pocket and pulled out a pack of matches. He had been secretly having a cigar now and then when Martha was nowhere in sight. Martha knew of his sometime habit and didn't approve but had kept her mouth shut waiting for the right time to bring it up. She was too afraid now and knew that this was not the time to say anything.

William lit a match. They were in a narrow passageway on the top step, hewn out of the hard packed dirt were 10 steps leading down to what seemed to end at a dirt wall. William's voice was just barely above a whisper as he called out, "Mary". No answer. The match went out. William struck another as they moved down one step. This time a bit louder, "Mary, are you down there?" William and Martha froze when a soft thud reached their ears - then nothing.

"Oh, my God, it must be Mary," Martha whispered. The dwindling flame touched Will's finger and he cried out. Martha jumped and grabbed wills arm. As he shook his hand due to the burn from the match, Martha fiercely told William to be quiet in case someone else was down there. Both stood silent for a few minutes, waiting to hear any other noises. Finally Martha called out in a loud voice, "Mary if you are down there, we are coming to get you." Again Will lit a match and the pair continued quickly down the last three steps and around the corner into a small room.

Blowing out the match and striking another, light was shed on the truth and each was surprised at what they saw. They were in a tiny room carved out of the earth measuring about 10 wide by 10 feet long and about 7 feet high. On one side of the room were floor to ceiling shelves loaded with all kinds of jars filled with peaches, blackberries, green beans and other things to eat. In one corner was a bushel basket full of potatoes and another basket half full of apples. One lone jar from the bottom shelf had slipped and fallen to the earth floor. Someone must have set it too close to the edge; the weight of the jar had eventually caused it to tip over and explained the sound of the soft thud that they had heard. "Well, I'll be. It's a canning room. Nothing sinister here," declared William.

"That's a relief, but it doesn't explain where Mary is. There is still something going on and I plan to find out what it is. I'm not afraid any more. I am angry and I want to know where my sister is. Let's go back to the Inn and find out."

Another match lighted the cramped passage for

the ascent to the top of the stairs and back out into the barn. Once more out in the open field covered by the cool light of the full moon, William and Martha, with new resolve, walked with determination back around to the front of the Inn, up the stairs and into the hall. They rounded the doorway into the lobby and abruptly stopped.

Chapter 10

Patricia was behind the massive counter in front of the row of keys hanging on the wall; a kerosene lamp sat next to her, reflecting the dancing flames on the polished surface. She cradled her head in her left hand as she bent over some paperwork that she was intently working on with a stub of a pencil. Hearing footsteps, Pat raised her head and smiled at the pair who had just entered the parlor.

Martha was the first to speak. "I demand to know where you have taken my sister."

"What?" The smile disappeared from Patricia's face. Frowning she replied, "What are you talking about?"

"Look, you can drop the act. I know what's in the attic and I have watched Tony and your so called little sister bewitch Mary into trusting all of you. I even saw your Aunt Katherine bringing out little men from the woods. So I know that all of you are up to no good and if you don't tell me where you have hidden my sister, I swear I will somehow find the cops and raid this God forsaken place."

Pat listened and watched as Martha continued, her voice getting louder and her face contorting in anger. Pat had no idea what Martha was upset about but it struck her as comical and she began to smile and then burst out laughing at the sight of Martha standing in her parlor waving her hands like a crazy person. The laughter caused Martha to stop in mid sentence. William stepped in closer to Pat and said in a slow deliberate voice, "I don't know what is so funny but we are very worried about Mary..... and, Martha has found some strange things that have us both questioning what is going on in this place."

"Whoa, I don't have the faintest idea of what either of you are talking about. Mary has been in our apartment for the past several hours visiting with Dora and my Aunt Katherine. What strange things are you talking about and why are you snooping in our attic? And, what do you mean you saw Aunt Katherine with little men? Have you both gone mad?"

William's boldness instantly ended and Martha felt the blood drain from her face as she steadied herself against Will's solid body. Was everything she had witnessed a figment of her imagination or was she just being drawn in closer to whatever evil was here? This was becoming a never ending terrible nightmare. Confused and embarrassed that she had poked around in the family's private area, Martha took a deep breath and decided she would be civil and hope to get to the bottom of what ever was going on.

Slowly and deliberately, Martha addressed Pat, "Look, I have been trying to find Mary for hours; she wasn't in her room, downstairs or on the porch. While I was searching for my sister, I started wandering up and down the halls, looking into all the rooms, and then I found the steps to the attic. I don't know what I was thinking. I just wanted to look everywhere in the hopes of finding Mary. But, once there, what I saw frightened and alarmed me."

"And, what did you see?" Pat stated, with a hint of sarcasm. "There is nothing in there that would scare anyone."

Martha thought she had her now. She knew that people don't keep the things she saw unless they are some kind of criminal or worse. Gaining courage from her indignation and self-righteousness, Martha decided to bring it all out in the open, "I saw all the weapons, the torture table and those photos of a dead boy. How do you explain that?"

Confusion furrowed Patricia's brow as she listened to Martha. What was she talking about? Then slowly, as understanding dawned, Pat smiled and began to laugh.

"I don't understand why you keep laughing. This is serious. I am telling you that I know what is in that attic. It is all there; everything points to terrible secrets. Who was that boy? Was he tortured? Why all the weapons? I saw the blood on the table and the pictures of that poor boy. You can't fool me. I know what I saw. And, and, your Aunt"...Martha's voice trembled... "your Aunt Katherine came out of the woods with little strange men, they were naked and dirty, and they had leaves for hair! I saw them shaking in her hands. How can you explain any of this?"

"Oh, I am sorry for laughing. But, you have twisted so many innocent things into such a weird conclusion that I just couldn't help myself. Look, why don't you and William join me for a cup of tea in our apartment. You can see that Mary is just fine and I will attempt to explain everything."

Martha and William, in spite of themselves, relaxed somewhat. Beginning to believe that Pat was telling them the truth, and that Mary was safe; they followed the Inn's owner toward the door next to the portrait of the stern gentleman that Martha had seen in the photo albums.

On the other side of the lobby was a well-equipped apartment. The first room contained an oversized flowered couch, a couple of easy chairs and a big square coffee table facing a small TV. Against an opposite wall was a large pine chest with an old record player sitting on top of several record albums next to a 50's style radio. In the corner was a coat tree with winter coats and a hat still hanging on the hooks. The living room opened into a short hall that contained an opened door revealing a half bath with a washer and dryer off to the right. The narrow hall then led to an enormous kitchen.

The kitchen was furnished with two electric stoves, a wall oven, an old farm style sink and two dishwashers . A large table surrounded by eight chairs stood in the middle of the kitchen next to a maple china cabinet full of the same white stoneware that dressed the dinning room tables. Martha realized that the door next to the china cabinet led into the massive dinning room that had first delighted her. A pine cabinet from years ago supported the sink with a Formica countertop in each side. The cabinets on the wall over the sink had glass fronts that exposed all sizes and colors of coffee mugs and other mismatched china. In one corner stood a metal baker's rack with a new microwave in the middle and an unbelievable amount of cookbooks on all the shelves. Next to the bakers rack on the back wall was a one of those walk in refrigerators that is standard equipment for most restaurants. In one corner was a pile of wood next to a small pot bellied stove that was warming the kitchen and simmering a tea kettle of hot water. Next to the refrigerator was a door that led to the basement. Martha was to find out later that the basement held a wonderful selection of wine and more of the same canned goods that were in the root cellar where they had just been.

Martha surveyed all of this in a few seconds. Then her eyes fell back on the table. There sitting at the table and talking to Dora and writing on a yellow legal pad was Mary. Tony was at the end of the table drinking a cup of instant coffee and thumbing through an old copy of field and stream. Aunt Katherine was sitting next to Mary.

Mary looked up as Martha entered. "Hi Sis, Will."

"Where have you been?" Martha demanded.

"What do you mean, where have I been?" Mary asked with a frown.

Martha's voice trembled and rose with each word, "I have been so worried. I couldn't find you anywhere. And I want to know what has been going on in this wretched place."

Mary sat back in her chair and with a look that contained embarrassment and indignation, stated, "Have you gone completely crazy big sister? Or are you on one of your self-righteous inquisitions?"

"It is not self-righteous to care for the welfare of my sister or to want to know about the weird things I have seen in this place. I noticed how you and Tony, if that's his real name, look at each other. I am telling you that you are making a big mistake getting involved with another man. I don't care how lonely you might be without your ladder climbing husband."

"Wait just a minute Martha." Mary insisted. "You

don't know what you are talking about. I can't believe you are still prying into my life. Besides, if I was doing anything that I would be sorry for, it's my life and none of your business. And, what do you mean weird things you have seen here? I think you have gone crazy and it looks like my so called brother-in-law is following in your footsteps."

"Now just a minute!" Will exclaimed.

Pat raised her voice just enough to be heard and interrupted, "If everyone would calm down, I am sure we can answer all questions. But for the life of me I can't understand how all of this came about." "Martha, Will, would you both please sit down and calmly tell me what is going on."

Will looked at Martha and she nodded. Slowly they each pulled out a chair and sat down across the table from Mary, Aunt Katherine and Dora. Pat continued, "Now Martha, please tell us exactly what you saw that frightened you so much."

"And do tell why you think that there is something going on between Tony and I, for heavens sake." Interjected Mary. "Yeah, I want to know too!" Tony quipped.

Martha sighed, "Well, I was worried about you being lonely, what with Donald gone so much and you seemed to hit it off so well with Tony that I naturally thought that there was a budding romance going on."

"Well, Miss priss!" Mary exclaimed, "I shouldn't have to defend myself but I will just this once, if you promise to stay out of my comings and goings from now on and trust that I am a decent person." Mary continued, "I shared with Tony my garden efforts and he showed me his rose garden and gave me some great tips. That is where I was when you were looking for me."

"But your room, it was unlocked and the bed was rumpled and your night bag was left open with half of your things on the dresser. You never leave a mess. I thought for sure you had been abducted."

Mary laughed. "Oh Martha, you take the most normal things and turn them in to downright evil. I left everything because I was in a hurry to see the roses before it got dark and I thought that I could tidy up the room later. Besides, no one was coming to visit me in my room, or so I thought."

Tony chimed in, "Your sister is an avid gardener. I am always interested in sharing with someone else who loves flowers like I do. And really that's all it was. Mary here was interested in seeing my rose garden and I was interested in showing off my skills." "Why, I have won several blue ribbons for my prize roses. Plus, I have a girlfriend in the next town that I am actually planning to propose to on her birthday next month. So you see, I am taken, thank you very much. No disrespect to Mary

"None taken", Mary smiled.

"Oh, Mary I am so sorry that I doubted you. I don't know how I let my imagination run away with me, always thinking the worst." Martha said more softly, "Believe me this is a lesson I won't soon forget."

"Well, I am glad to hear that." Mary replied. "However, it will take some time for me to believe that you really mean what you are saying now."

Martha, much more subdued, still wanted to know what had been going on between her sister and Dora, not to mention all the stuff that she saw in the attic. She cautiously asked, "Another thing that had me going was when I opened your door at one point and found Dora sitting on the bench under the window with your head in her lap. I mean, that was sort of weird. I have never known you to get close to someone so quickly. I really thought that somehow Dora had bewitched you or something."

This time Dora laughed, "You really are suspicious." She commented, "I will tell you exactly why I was in Mary's room and what I was doing." "I had come up to the room to deliver the kerosene lamp and matches to your sister and found her crying. I sat down with her and hugged her. When she stopped crying she just naturally laid her head in my lap. She was upset about going to the family reunion alone when there are always couples and wished that she and her husband could spend more time together. She felt especially sad that she had lost the sister that she was close to and she told me that she had never felt that you understood her. I shared with her my own lost love and we wound up crying together."

"When you opened the door, I smiled at you because I was glad Mary had a sister that she could confide in. I encouraged her to share with you her fear that she would lose you if she got too close to you, like she lost her baby sister. I told Mary how Pat has always listened to my tales of woe and still stayed there beside me. I mean that is what sisters are for, don't you think? To help each other." "After we each had a good cry, I invited Mary to the kitchen and we have been swapping recipes. She just gave me a recipe for her lemon cake, which sounds wonderful."

"Okay, so I was wrong about Tony's and Dora's intentions." Martha replied, and I am glad that both of you befriended my sister. I guess there are explanations for everything else. Although I can't for the life of me figure out what some of those could be,"

Martha still feeling awkward and shameful about all that she had already heard, that explained so much, took a breath and swallowed to build up her nerve to ask about what was left that she believed couldn't be explained away. (A part of her still believed that something bad had happened in that house even if these people hadn't done it)

"Could you all humor me for a bit longer and put the remainder of my fears to rest about the other things I saw." "I mean, think about it, guns and knives on the wall, a blood soaked table, pictures of coffins and people in black. You have to admit all of that is pretty weird." "And," she continued, with another breath to steady her thumping heart, "I swear, I saw Aunt Katherine coming out of the woods holding what looked like little men that were alive and shaking. Can you explain any of that?" Martha asked.

Chapter 11

Pat stood up and walked over to the pot bellied stove. Grabbing a pot holder hung on the wall next to the stove, she picked up the kettle and approached the table. She handed Will and Martha a box of assorted tea bags and mugs from the center of the table next to a small jar of instant coffee. After the pair choose their tea, Pat began pouring the steaming liquid into each mug. "Here have some tea. This will take awhile."

Sitting down, Pat began to tell the story of Summer Hill Inn. "I grew up in this house before it was an Inn. In the 1800's, many people owned similar southern plantations. This house was left over from my great-grandfather who had several hundred acres and many slaves to till the land. After he died the estate went to my grandfather and then later to my father and his siblings.

My father was the oldest of three sons and two daughters. He wanted the house for his new wife and the large family he hoped to have. He met with his brothers and sisters and they agreed to let him have the house. They sold off most of the land and the money was divided between them, with my father getting the house and the 50 acres surrounding it, instead of cash."

"I was born shortly after my parents moved into the house and then in a few years came Dora and then our brother, Tommy. He was born when I was nine and Dora was four. We loved living here. Daddy added the barn and we had a couple of horses and a cow and lots of chickens. There is a tree house that my father built for us behind the barn in a very old large Maple tree. We spent hours up there planning adventures and making believe we were explorers looking for treasure. We had great fun in the woods where we built a secret clubhouse near a small creek. It was a wonderful life. We were able to roam to our heart's content never worrying about the things kids have to worry about today."

"The picture you saw of the young woman with a baby was my mother holding Tommy. He was a sweet child and a delight to us all. He was cute and funny and we all loved him, especially daddy. My father loved him so much, that he indulged Tommy at every opportunity, much to the chagrin of my mother. Dora and I never minded very much because Tommy never acted spoiled and he was generous and loving to us. Plus, my father was good natured and kind to my mother and his daughters. It was just that Tommy held a special place in his heart."

"Tommy was fascinated with weapons of all sorts and he particularly liked knives and swords from the orient. One year when he was four, mother joined a foreign student exchange program and we had a 16 year old from Sweden live with us for the whole school year. Tommy was awed by our new house guest and spent hours watching him practice his Judo moves and he tagged along when Tor went to practice and to the tournaments."

After Tor went back home to Sweden, Tommy begged to join the Yellow Hill Judo club two towns over and once again daddy couldn't refuse him. My father got very involved and took Tommy to all of his practices and tournaments. Dora and I often went to tournaments to cheer Tommy on. My mother only went a few times to watch Tommy; she was always afraid that Tommy would get hurt so she stayed away after the first few months and trusted that daddy would take care of her baby. Tommy started collecting the different weapons you saw on the shelf in the attic when he was about 10. He did all kinds of odd jobs, mostly for our father, but also he did some jobs like mowing the grass, for some of our neighbors that live down the road a bit." He would find something special, in a catalog that he had sent away for, and then save all of his money to buy the knife or sword. My father collected the guns. Collecting weapons was an interest they both shared. We were always having the UPS truck or the mail bringing us something. "

"What about the table? Martha questioned. "It looked like dried blood at one end."

"Oh, that. That is an old stained table I bought at a yard sale years ago and I thought I would refinish it. It is solid oak and I thought it would go great in the kitchen or as a table for a large group of Inn guests. I think that I just forgot about it. I am always so busy with other projects that I just haven't gotten around to doing it." Pat explained.

Martha, now quiet, understood. "Thank you for telling me all of this." "I'm so sorry, I think I just put a bunch of things together that were easily explained and let my imagination run away with me." "I am still curious about the coffin. Do you mind telling me what happened?"

Pat smiled at Martha and the rest of her guests, "Well, let me continue where I was in the story, in order to give you the whole picture. We haven't talked about this for a long time and we should."

"Tommy stayed in Judo for several years and brought home several trophies. He also did something called mixed martial arts until he became a teenager. When he was 14, Tommy started asking for a motorcycle."

"My mother was fit to be tied and told him there

was no way that she would let him get a motorcycle. Tommy worked on daddy for about 6 months, promising that he would be careful and would only drive it around our property. Daddy caved in and told mother that Tommy would be careful and wouldn't be driving it on the highway. She finally gave in." Pat concluded. "Where daddy couldn't refuse Tommy, mother couldn't refuse daddy."

"Tommy kept to his promise for the next seven or eight months and mother relaxed and stopped her anxious comments to him to be careful every time he went riding. I guess one day he got tired of always being confined to the trails he had made on our land and decided to go on the road below the gravel driveway where your car is stranded. It wasn't the highway and I think he felt he was still keeping his promise. None of us knew he was there and he certainly didn't have permission from our parents to leave our property. He must have just pulled on to the road when the delivery truck hit him. We are not sure how it happened but he skidded into a UPS truck that was bringing a package from the Knife Works catalog to our house. He was knocked off the motorcycle and landed in the ditch. He was pretty banged up but alive. The UPS driver left Tommy and ran up the gravel road to tell us what happened. I called 911 while the truck driver, Dora, Mom and Dad raced down the road back to Tommy.

The police and EMS came. I got down the road just as they were putting Tommy in the ambulance. . After they took Tommy to the hospital, we piled into dad's station wagon and drove the thirty miles to the hospital in town. Tommy had a broken leg and a concussion but we all thought he would make it. After a few days, Tommy got sick in the hospital with a virus. He was running a low fever and complained of his throat hurting. It was late and the nurse called the doctor with his symptoms. The doctor felt he would be ok until morning rounds and told the nurse to give him a couple of Tylenol for his fever and sore throat. That night Tommy died. His throat swelled and closed, cutting off his air. We will never know why the nurse didn't find him until the next morning."

"We were shocked. I remember my mother and father asking God why he took their son at such a young age. Dora cried every night; I just kept my sorrow in and tried to comfort her. My parents never got over losing Tommy. Mother moved into Tommy's room and refused to come out. She wouldn't speak to daddy or us. We took meals to her and she would eat a bite or two and push the rest away. She died several months later, I guess from a broken heart. Daddy tried to keep everything together but he lost his easy going spirit and became stern and critical."

"Yes, Father did change." Dora piped up, "and I

got the worse of it since I was the next youngest one. I was very close to my father when I was little and I was just a little jealous when Tommy came on the scene. He was a boy after all and so cute and he had such a sweet disposition. It was as if Tommy replaced me. I mean daddy was still good to me but it wasn't the same. After Tommy died, I did get all the attention from my father that I had wanted but now the attention was constant. He became controlling and strict." Dora bowed her head and continued somewhat under her breath. "I think that is why I fell in love with a Bible salesman so quickly after Tommy died."

Mary looked at Dora with concern, "What happened?"

Dora raised her head and looked back at Mary, "Remember I told you that I had lost the love of my life and how my sister helped me to get over it. Well, I was talking about Johnny."

Dora straightened in her chair and seemed to transform from a frumpy child woman to an adult with an important story to tell. "I was 16 when Tommy died. It was awful how it affected my mother and daddy. Daddy was always protective of his children but now he wouldn't let me out of his sight. I wasn't allowed to go anywhere without Pat and daddy wouldn't let me date. It was as if he thought that unless he watched me like a hawk, I might die too. That summer after the funeral, a young man from the next town came to the house selling bibles. He was 19 and was raising money to go to college in the fall. He wanted to get a degree in business management. He was handsome and sweet and he liked me. His name was John Anderson. I fell hard for him."

"A few days later, he came to the high school to find me and we started seeing each other. I would sneak out at night to meet with him. We spent hours talking and saw each other for over a year without my daddy knowing. We realized that we needed to tell my father and also to ask him if we could date until I finished school and then we wanted to get married. John was the love of my life. He was kind and he had a lot of ambition to make something of himself. At the time, I just knew that daddy would see how wonderful Johnny was and would give his consent."

"On Friday, John came to the school. He found me before I got on the bus and wanted to talk to me about how we were going to approach my father. We made plans for John to come to the house on a Sunday night after my father had rested from working all week. John and I planned everything he was going to say to daddy and he practiced with me that night when I left the house and met him in the garden." "When the big day came, I was so nervous that daddy knew something was up because he kept asking me what was wrong. I just kept telling him that nothing was the matter. I picked up a magazine and sat near the door to the hall pretending to read, while waiting to hear the front door bell."

"That night, the bell had just barely rung when I jumped up and ran to the door and let Johnny in. He came into the parlor and introduced himself. At first daddy didn't remember him until John reminded him about how he had first met our family when he was selling bibles the year before. My father told Johnny that he did remember, shook his hand and asked him what he was selling now. John nervously said that he wasn't selling anything but had come to talk to him. Daddy seemed confused. He sat back down in his chair, motioned Johnny to sit down. My father just stared at him and when Johnny didn't say anything Daddy told him to go ahead and speak his piece. Johnny took a deep breath to steady himself and then started with his prepared speech."

"It didn't go at all the way we had planned. I think Daddy had an inkling of why Johnny was there. Before John had a chance to finish, daddy started screaming at him and forbid him to ever see me again. John ran out of the house and I never saw him again." "It was terrible." Dora angrily wiped away a tear as it traveled down her face. "I heard later that he met some girl in college and they married." "I don't think he ever cared for me the way I cared for him or he would have fought harder for me or at least waited until I was 18 to rescue me."

Mary took Dora's hand and squeezed it. Dora smiled at Mary and said, "All of that is under the bridge now. I don't want or need anyone to love me. I have my sister and my aunt Katherine and I am kept very busy cooking for this crowd and for our summer guests." Brightening, Dora reverted back to her original childlike state and declared, "I can hardly wait to try Mary's lemon cake. I bet the guests will love it. Dessert is my favorite thing!"

Martha leaned back into her chair and sipped her tea. All of her bravado was gone. Will had been quiet as the others talked. He felt enormous relief to find out the real story and sadness for this family that had endured so much. He also chided himself to be a stronger leader for his family and to bring a sense of reason to the mix when his wife went on one of her tangents instead of him falling in line with her exaggerated beliefs. He said a quick prayer and asked God for guidance and wisdom.

Aunt Katherine cleared her throat and began to speak. "So missy, you thought I was doing some sort of magic or some other kind of evil when you watched Tony and I come from the barn."

Martha blushed and said, "I did let my imagination

get away with me, didn't I? I swear though, I did see you come out of the woods with two little men in your hands. And, they must have been alive because they were moving. How can you explain that?"

Aunt Katherine chuckled, "You live in North Carolina and you haven't ever heard of or seen ginseng? It grows wild in the woods and I often go and pick it. We dry it and sell it. It's worth a lot of money to many who think it has healing properties. It is one way that I can make a little money for personal items and then I don't have to beg from my nieces, who have enough to worry about. It's my way of earning my keep."

"But they looked human and they moved," Martha protested.

"That is how ginseng grows." Aunt Katherine explained. "Its roots often look like legs and arms, and I was shaking the dirt off so I guess it did look like they were alive but I assure you that they were not and that they are nothing more than highly prized plants."

"The government controls the harvesting of ginseng on federal property so it isn't depleted but these plants grow on our own property so I can pick it and use it for myself." Martha, feeling ashamed apologized.

"All is forgiven," Pat replied, as she stood up and began clearing the table. "And now it is getting rather late and I have a lot of work to do tomorrow. I am sure the electric company and the phone company will be here bright and early ready to get us up and running."

Mary stood up, "You're right, it is late and I'm tired. It has been a very eventful day. See you all in the morning." She came over to the other side of the table and kissed Martha on the cheek. Whispering in Martha's ear, Mary said, "Please trust me in the future, sis. I would never hurt Donald or do anything against God. I may not always talk about God the way you do, but believe me, I do my best to follow Him."

As Martha watched Mary leave the kitchen, she said a silent prayer, asking God to forgive her for not trusting her sister and to strengthen their relationship. William looked at Martha and signaled that it was time to go. She agreed and they both rose from their chairs, said goodnight to their hosts and left the kitchen.

Chapter 12

Nothing more was said that night. All of them were weary from the day's events and all slept soundly. The next morning Martha, Will and Mary awoke to the sound of trucks driving up the gravel road into the parking lot and noises coming from downstairs.

Martha woke first and leaned over and kissed her husband. She was thankful that he hadn't upbraided her about her foolish actions. Will opened his eyes and smiled at Martha. He reached over to her and pulled her close. She melted against his strength and delighted in his warmth. How she loved to snuggle in the early morning. It was the time of the day that she felt particularly safe and loved. William also loved these quiet morning moments before the day began and today he felt much stronger and more in God's will for him as a husband. God had been teaching him how to love his wife as Christ loved the church and he was learning to recognize His leading.

Will and Martha each washed their face and brushed their teeth in the little sink in the tiny bathroom. They dressed quickly and went down stairs.

The aroma of bacon and coffee met them as they walked into the parlor. Pat was there and she invited them to sit in the dining room for breakfast. As they entered the dining room, flames were dancing in the enormous fire place, chasing away the morning chill. Mary was sitting at one of the tables close to the fire sipping coffee. William and Martha walked up to her table that was set for four.

"Hi sleepy heads." Mary cheerfully greeted them. "I have been up and about for over an hour. Pat just said breakfast is almost ready. The power is on and the phones are working. Let's eat and then call a mechanic to fix the car." Martha and William eagerly agreed to Mary's proposal. Pulling out chairs they sat down and sipped ice water which was already by their places.

Shortly, Dora brought in hot coffee, scrambled eggs, bacon, sausage, creamy grits and a basket full of freshly baked biscuits. Husband and wife and sister-in-law enjoyed the hearty breakfast. When they were finished, the trio went into the parlor in order to call someone to fix their car. Patricia was already on the phone and told them she would make the call while they packed.

Back in their room, Martha told Will that she had learned a valuable lesson. She shared with her husband that she was going to be extra careful about expecting the worst and about thinking that she somehow had the responsibility to be involved in other people's lives. Martha confessed that she was going to start asking herself when she was tempted to intervene, to question whose business it was before she jumped in with advice or other forms of meddling. William hugged Martha. He told her that he was glad to hear her plan and that he had also made some decisions. He shared with her his own revelation of how God was teaching him how to be a better husband. He told Martha that he realized that he needed to be better able to quell her fears by helping her to look at situations in a realistic light. He said that he wanted to be the kind of husband that she could trust and lean on. Martha Hugged William back and kissed him. She silently thanked God for William and for helping each of them to learn such valuable lessons. Martha thought of her favorite bible verse and quoted it to William. "I am again reminded of what Paul said to the Romans: "All things work together for those that love God and are called for His Purpose." "Ah, Yes," William agreed. "Romans 8:28. It is totally amazing how God uses so many different things to help us grow."

Bags in hand, William and Martha came down the stairs to the parlor. Mary came down the stairs a few moments later and joined her sister and brother-in-law as they walked up to the desk. Aunt Katherine was in her favorite rocking chair knitting a scarf of blue and purple yarn. Pat put down the phone and told the threesome that a mechanic was on his way. Will gave Patricia their room keys and asked for the bill.

Pat told them that there wasn't any charge since they weren't officially opened. "And, besides," she said, "I have never been so entertained in my whole life." William and Martha thanked Pat for her generosity and told Pat they would have to come back next fall to celebrate their anniversary and hoped they could have the same room. Dora came out of the kitchen. She hugged Mary and told her to promise to stay in touch. Mary agreed and thanked Dora for all the southern recipes that she had given her.

Aunt Katherine stood up and told the group good bye and to stay safe. Martha went over to Aunt Katherine, gave her a hug and said. "Thank you for your kindness Aunt Katherine." Aunt Katherine smiled and sat back down and picked up her knitting. Will Martha and Mary left the parlor and opened the door to the porch. Descending down the stairs they all started talking at once.

"I can't believe that Pat didn't charge us for our stay, Mary started. "I know," Martha chimed in. Let's hope we can get our car to start so that we can get to Raleigh today." Will agreed, "The mechanic is meeting us at the end of the road, so maybe it isn't anything serious and we can be on our way sooner rather than later."

SUMMER HILL INN

The threesome noted that the ruts in the gravel road had been smoothed out and all the previous puddles had dried. Tony was weed eating the edge of the road. He saw the group as they passed him and he waved good bye. At the end of the short drive Martha noticed that the Summer Hill Inn sign had been righted and now pointed appropriately up the hill, seeming a lot less sinister than a day earlier.

A tow truck with the words "We Tow 'em & We Fix 'em" written in bright red letters on an off white background was waiting for them. A young man was leaning on the truck. When he saw the group come down from the gravel road, he stood up and walked over to the car. William got to the car first. The tow truck owner put out his hand and shaking Will's hand, stated that his name was Randy and asked what the problem was with the car.

"I don't know," Will said, "we were lost so we pulled over to look at our map and when I tried to start the car again, we only heard a clicking sound." "Hmmm," Randy replied, "get in and release the hood and I will take a look at it." Will did as he was told. He got in the car, left the door open and pulled the latch releasing the lock on the hood. Randy pulled up the metal and hooked the rod in place under the hood. He hollered at William to turn the key. Will did so and the motor roared to life.

Will, surprised, got out of the car and stood by Randy, "I can't explain it. It wouldn't start at all yesterday."

"Well, no problem, it seems to be working fine now." The mechanic said, as he lowered the hood into place.

"How much do I owe you?" Will asked. "Not a dime, didn't do a thing." Randy responded. "I was planning to go up the hill and see my friends at the Inn anyway. If I am real nice to Pat and Aunt Katherine, I might be able to get a big bowl of Dora's warm blackberry cobbler with vanilla ice cream melting on top. Ya'll have a nice day."

With those words, Randy walked back to his truck, and got behind the wheel. Closing the door he started the engine and turned the pickup a sharp right to face the gravel road. Putting the tow truck into gear, he drove up the road and out of site.

"Wow," exclaimed Martha, "I am so glad the car is working." "Me too," echoed Mary as she opened the back door and slid into the seat. "Let's get going." stated Martha as she climbed into the passenger's seat. William got behind wheel, closed the door and moved the gear out of park and into drive. He slowly turned around to face the way they had originally traveled on the wrong road to get back on the highway to Raleigh.

As William drove, each passenger shared the

lessons that they had learned during their stay at the Inn. When it was Martha's turn she told her family how she had realized that she still tended to be controlling and had forgotten that when she was faced with things that made her fearful, to go in prayer to God and to trust that God did a much better job than she ever could to make everything ok in all situations. She apologized to her husband for not listening to his insistence that she was letting her imagination get the best of her and promised to try to listen to his voice of reason in the future. Turning toward the backseat, she apologized to Mary, for her suspicious accusations of wrong doing, and promised to stop being a busy body and to trust that her sister was an adult and able to make good decisions. Mary reached her hand up to her sister and touched her shoulder.

"It's ok, Martha, I love you and understand that you have a hard time letting go. I will ask God to help you in my prayers." I do pray you know, and He listens."

Martha replied, "I'm sorry Mary, I guess I just haven't gotten to know you and have just assumed things about you. I won't do that anymore. Let's see each other more so that we can get to know each other better."

"You've got a deal, Martha." Replied Mary, "Maybe

we can go antiquing sometime and maybe we could visit each other more. We are only 4 hours away from each other. It wouldn't be that hard for us to get together more. I would love your company when Don is on the road."

"Great idea," Martha replied, "when this trip is over, we can look at our calendars and make plans." "Maybe I can spend a night with you now and then in the summer when I don't have to work."

Mary agreed. "That's a great idea!" We could go more places and have more fun that way and you wouldn't have to rush back home so quickly."

Will smiled listening to his wife and sister-in-law. He said a quick prayer, thanking God for not only taking care of them but also answering his prayer for his wife and sister to come closer to each other.

As they drove away from Summer Hill Inn and all that it represented, William, with a new strength said, "I don't know if evil is personified in witches spells or in the worship of demons, I do know that the human heart is always in danger of devising its own evil and I am sure that Satan is able to help the flesh in committing all kinds of sinful actions. We need to be forever on guard against our own tendency to slide into wickedness while trusting that God loves us and takes care of us. We know so little and we can get into all kinds of trouble when we believe we have arrived and then become complacent or believe that we know it all and forget who is in charge.

"Amen," Martha replied, and in her heart she thanked God for his patience with her and for teaching her the lessons she had learned at Summer Hill Inn.

Settling back into the softness of the car seat for the drive to Raleigh, Martha watched the scenery glide by. Thinking of her relatives and the upcoming funeral, she felt she had a new understanding of the pain that they would be feeling. She hoped she would be a comfort and a blessing to each one, especially her mother.

Epilog

"This is the verdict: light has come into the world, but men loved darkness instead of light because their deeds were evil. Everyone who does evil hates the light, and will not come into the light for fear that his deeds will be exposed. But whoever lives by the truth comes into the light, so that is may be seen plainly that what he has done has been done though God." John 19-21

"Then you will know the truth and the truth will set you free." John 8:32

www.ingramcontent.com/pod-product-compliance
Lightning Source LLC
LaVergne TN
LVHW041706060526
838201LV00043B/606